SHURI

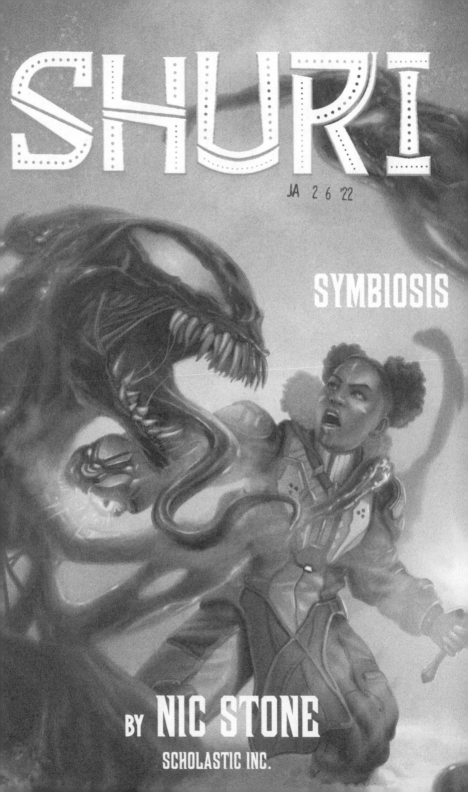

FOR MY BELOVED NIGEL,
WHO MADE ME FEEL LIKE I COULD FLY
(SYMBIOTIC WEBBING OPTIONAL).

ISBN 978-1-338-76653-0

1 2021

Printed in the U.S.A.   23

First printing 2022

Book design by Katie Fitch

PROLOGUE

And then Shuri is flying.

It's the forward momentum—and the drop of her stomach into her ankles—that coax her eyelids open . . .

She's soaring through the mountains, plunging down, then up, then forward, and again . . . down, back up, forward. A perfect parabola with each swing. There's the Jabari fertile plateau with all its varieties of ice-dusted produce. And then the city, dark and silent as a tomb . . . Thick off-white ropes shoot from her wrist and attach themselves to high cliffs and mountain peaks that she swoops by.

It's nothing short of exhilarating.

A voice rings in her head: *Ah! Princess see now! Feel good! Not monster!*

You can say that again, Shuri thinks as she drops into the next arc. *I never want this to end . . .*

But a few swings later, her feet are landing on a tiny ledge in the face of a cliff wall. And then she's crawling up, up, up, on her fingertips and toes.

When she reaches the top and looks around, she almost can't believe what she's seeing: her beloved nation stretched out before her. There's Birnin S'Yan, Birnin Zana with the Necropolis just outside it. There's the Sacred Mound. The baobab plain. Birnin Azzaria, Birnin Bashenga, Birnin Djata, Birnin T'Chaka.

And there are the mountains she's standing in. The Jabari village and M'Baku's Ice Fortress.

This is *her* kingdom full of *her* people. And looking out over all of it, Shuri knows beyond a shadow of a doubt that it is *her* job to both protect what is here *and* do good in the wider world with it.

Perhaps even in the universe.

MISSION LOG

WE HAVE ALMOST DONE IT.

Today K'Marah and I were granted an audience with the king and queen. And let me tell you: Needing an appointment and "approval" to speak with my own mother and melon-headed older brother was . . . Well, as K'Marah smugly put it, "Looks like you got a heaping spoonful of what the Americans call *humble pie* today, Princess."

She wasn't incorrect.

However, my sense of dignity was restored once K'Marah and I completed our presentation and were met with impressed looks from my nation-leading relatives AND an agreement from T'Challa that—if we manage to get that Fury man and his organization on board with our plan—Wakanda will fully fund the enterprise we proposed.

Which is the only way we'd be able to achieve our aim: utilize Lady Nirvana's Hive to host a series of two-week S.T.E.A.M. residencies (we intend to add an arts wing) for budding young scientists and creatives who need the space and resources to pursue a large-scale project or investigate a hypothesis that requires intensive focus.

Since freeing all those girls from the Hive some months ago, K'Marah, Riri, and I have worked tirelessly to expand that network and learn about OTHER girls who might be interested in spending some time in what I'm fairly certain is actual Experimentation Heaven.

Hate to say it, but even my quintessential "state-of-the-art" lab seems antiquated in comparison to the Hive. And I would be telling a lie if I said I hadn't considered that this initiative would involve ME going back there. Might as well make the most of the place . . .

My hope is that with so many innovation-driven minds gathered in one location—and NOT under the influence of auditory and olfactory hypnosis—we will be able to help one another along in our scientific and technological pursuits.

I know I could certainly use some additional minds to assist *me* with a few problems that need solutions.

Which reminds me, I must tweak the security dome algorithm and figure out how to fix the hole right above the mountains that comprise the Jabari-Lands.

I wonder if the lack of technology there is somehow creating some sort of digital vacuum . . . I bet if we were in one of our residencies, someone at the Hive would be able to tell me instantly.

The good news: Riri has already "touched base," as she put it, with Mr. Fury and his consortium: S.H.I.E.L.D. She called very excited this afternoon to tell me that the Iron fellow is interested in becoming a sponsor and wants to provide some of the tech equipment himself.

So here's to Run-The-World Camp.

Now I just hope I'll be able to fix this dome-hole problem as soon as possible. I still sometimes dream about that time the princess of Narobia made an invasion attempt and almost succeeded. Things have been relatively calm here since—though I can't say the same is true for the rest of the world. So, better safe than sorry. There are more people out there who know of our existence than I'm expressly comfortable with. Especially now that we are going to be working with Mr. Fury and his S.H.I.E.L.D.

No telling when someone will figure out *where* we are . . . and try to come in.

1

INTRUSION

Despite knowing that what she's feeling isn't actually happening, Princess Shuri is so *shook* by the sense of being covered in spiders, she wonders if it's possible to faint when you're asleep.

It's not real, Shuri, she says to her snoozing self (so bizarre). *This is merely one of those* lucid dream *things Kocha M'Shindi warned you about.*

And the Kocha had warned Shuri that lucid dreams—the type where she's fully aware that she's dreaming—were a common side effect of "immersion phobia-therapy." It's the Kocha's latest form of torture the princess has to undergo as part of her Panther training. "We must eliminate all potential hindrances to quick action," she said as she shoved Shuri into a small, dimly lit room that had a dozen tarantulas scurrying around within it.

The princess could have sworn she would cease to exist right then and there.

Interestingly enough, the furry, many-legged creatures seemed even keener on staying away from the princess than she was on staying away from them. Which, when she thought about it, made quite a bit of sense: She was fully capable of crushing the things with a single stomp. How would *she* feel if a creature hundreds of times her size was looming over her?

Better yet, how would she feel if said creature seemed to *fear* her?

How silly she suddenly felt about being afraid.

And yet . . .

"Great Bast, great *Bast*," she pants. "Okay, okay, okay. Not *real*, Shuri. They aren't *real*."

But they *feel* real. Far, far too real.

In this lucid dream, there are far more than twelve of the hairy little creatures. So many more, the princess couldn't begin to count them if she tried.

And unfortunately, in this dream-space, they aren't

running away. Quite the opposite. Shuri is standing with her feet planted shoulder-width apart and her arms stretched out to her sides, and the tarantulas are *all over* her. Crawling up and down her arms and legs, scuttling around her midsection.

She's breathing, but just barely.

"Not real, not real, not *real*. Hey, actual Shuri, wouldn't be a bad idea to wake up now! I think we're good on the whole phobia immersion concept!"

How do I get out *of this thing?* the princess wonders, trying to lift her arms or wiggle her toes. Movement is impossible. Her limbs feel as heavy as the condensed core of a collapsed star. Even *within* the dream, she's frozen in place, despite the fact that her shoulders are beginning to ache from holding her arms aloft.

She wants to scream but is afraid that if she opens her mouth, the eight-legged furballs will crawl right in. Down her throat, into her belly, and . . .

Her body shudders in her sleep.

"Mmmmmmm!" She hums within the dream, feeling her heart rate rise. (At least she thinks it's rising . . . can one really tell when not actually conscious?)

There's the sudden, faint *WHOOP* of a siren from somewhere behind the princess. She twists around on instinct and a bunch of the creeper-crawlies go flying.

"Huh," she says, surprised. But now she has an idea: With her arms outstretched, the princess begins to spin. Slowly at first, then faster and faster until she's basically a human centrifuge with tarantulas flying off her in every direction—

The siren sounds again. Louder this time. Startles Shuri so bad, she trips over her feet and goes sprawling. The spiders swarm.

"Ahhh!" she yells, attempting to scramble back to her feet.

"Shuri!"

"Great Bast, are they *talking* to me now?" Her voice cracks like a pubescent boy's, and she claps a hand over her mouth.

"Shuri! You must wake!"

Wait a second . . . The princess looks around, but her pause has given the creatures enough time to almost completely overtake her.

The siren howls louder.

"SHURI!" The whole room begins to shake, and dream Shuri *does* open her mouth to scream—

Her *actual* mouth opens, too, apparently. And as her eyes fly open, a hand clamps down over it.

◈◈◈◈

It takes Shuri far longer than she's expressly comfortable with to recognize the figure standing over her. It's the queen mother. Looking just as terrified as Shuri feels.

"Do. Not. Scream," Mother says, barely above a whisper. "We must get to the bunker immediately."

The *bunker*??

Shuri's shock must be evident in her eyes because then the queen mother says, "No questions now, Shuri. This isn't the time. Understand?"

The princess nods, too shaken to do anything but agree.

"I'm going to take my hand away now," Mother continues.

And she does. Slowly.

Shuri gulps but keeps her lips sealed.

"Come," Mother says. "Quickly."

Without a word, Shuri follows the queen mother out of her quarters and into the hallway where Nakia, Ayo, and two other Dora Milaje are waiting. It's more dimly lit than usual. Well, except for the brightly flashing fluorescent lights every few meters.

Which is when Shuri realizes the siren is still going off.

It's the palace alarm.

"Mother—"

"Not now, Shuri!" the queen hisses.

Instead of taking a left once they reach the main

hallway, the pair of Wakandan royals—in pajamas—and their guards go right. Shuri opens her mouth to speak again, but Ayo, seeming to sense what Shuri is thinking, cuts the princess a look, so Shuri thinks better of it.

Soon, they are entering the queen's quarters. "This way," Nakia says, heading straight for Ramonda's cavernous dressing chambers.

Shuri looks up at the portraits of all the former queens as if to say: *Do* you *all have any idea what's going on?*

None of them respond.

As they approach what is clearly a wall, Shuri is tempted to pipe up and ask if she's being punk'd. She learned of the concept—basically a synonym for "pranked," but with cameras involved—from an old television show K'Marah introduced her to on PantherTube.

But then Ayo lays her palm against a random spot on the golden wallpaper . . . and a panel slides open, revealing a lit corridor beyond.

Now the princess wouldn't be able to speak if she tried.

This isn't the first time Shuri has been made privy to some secret passageway in the palace, and she is no less irritated than she was the first time it happened.

Mere months ago, Mother led her through a hidden doorway like this one—and directly to her *grounded* doom after she snuck out of the country for a second time. And it didn't matter that she'd been on a mission to save the lives of countless missing girls.

She shudders at the memory.

However, after descending a long staircase into a narrow hallway and what seems like an interminable walk, they step into a space the princess hasn't seen since she was six years old (which was when its existence was made known to her, though getting there by secret-passageway-through-Mother's-closet is certainly new): the palace bunker.

Shuri almost stops dead: It's been almost eight years, and the interior hasn't undergone a single upgrade. Her last time here, they were testing a new national security system shortly after Baba was killed by that Vibranium-hungry wannabe jerk, Ulysses Klaw. And her first thought upon entering back *then* was *Sheesh, this place is rather pedestrian.* Mother had used that term a few days earlier to describe the unadorned dress the princess wanted to wear to some fancy dinner with the tribal leaders. So she knew it was fitting: The bunker was a four-walled room with nothing inside but a long steel table with a dozen or so very uncomfortable chairs; a miniature refrigerator and basket full of unperishables; and a wall of ancient television monitors that served as security screens.

So *un*-Wakandan. Especially considering that the woman who woke Shuri in the dead of night is wearing a shimmering teal three-piece sleeping gown set that includes a matching head wrap.

As the queen walks over to turn on the wall of technological dinosaurs—sorry, *monitors*—two Dora Milaje shut and seal the door. Despite the befuddling circumstances, this triggers a memory for the princess: Her other time here, she'd been fascinated by that door. Knocked on it and everything. "It's a titanium-Vibranium alloy," one of the guards told her. "Completely impenetrable and virtually indestructible. Queen N'Yami created it before marrying your father. The floor, ceiling, and walls are all lined with it as well." Back then, it made Shuri smile to learn that something integral to the safety of Wakanda had been created by a woman: T'Challa's birth mother.

She's not smiling now, though.

"Mother—"

"Sit, Shuri," the queen says, pointing her daughter to the seat farthest from the door.

"But, Mother, why—"

"Still not the time, sweetheart."

As she plops down—with Nakia sliding into the

chair at her right, and Ayo at her left—and the adrenaline subsides, Shuri's vision blurs and her eyelids begin to droop. Of course whatever is going on would happen mere hours after T'Challa left to join some mission with Mr. Fury and a group of American Super Heroes who call themselves the Avengers (fairly *brutal* name, if you ask the princess).

So very sleepy.

"I still don't *understand*," Ramonda says, snapping the princess awake. "How could this have happened?" She rotates to face the Dora and her daughter. "Our grounds guards undergo *extensive* tactical training, do they not?"

"They do, Your Majesty," Ayo says.

"So explain this to me!" She throws a hand up to gesture at the monitors.

Shuri looks . . . and sees nothing. Like zero movement on any of the twenty or so screens.

"I . . ." Nakia and the other Dora glance around at each other. "I'm sorry we don't have an explanation as of yet, my queen. We will review the footage—"

"And what will that *solve*, Nakia?" Mother snaps.

A small well of panic opens in Shuri's chest. She's never seen Mother this . . . unhinged. (For her, at least.)

"We understand your frustrations, Your Majesty.

You have our word that we will work tirelessly until we get to the bottom of this—"

"The bottom of *what*?" Shuri exclaims, not really meaning to, but clearly unable to resist.

She and the queen lock eyes, and Shuri's mouth snaps shut. The princess holds her breath, awaiting what is sure to be quite the tongue-lashing . . .

But it doesn't come.

Instead, Queen Ramonda collapses into a chair.

Shuri's not sure which is more frightening: seeing Mother *wig out*, as K'Marah would put it, or seeing all the fight go out of her like a wilting heart-shaped herb plant. "Mother?"

"We've had a break-in, Shuri," comes Ramonda's defeated reply.

Which . . . *"Huh?"*

"You heard me correctly," Ramonda says. "There is an intruder in the palace."

2
ESCAPE

This time, Shuri is snatched from slumber by shouting. *When had she fallen asleep?*

"What do you mean, *GONE*?"

Mother.

The princess quickly shuts her eyes. She knows how *this* typically goes: As soon as the adults realize she's awake, they will shift to hushed tones and/or end the conversation. But Shuri *needs* to know what is happening. She might totally lose it if she doesn't get some information.

After dropping the whole *intruder* bomb, the queen

mother had lapsed into silence. The Dora started discussing what they knew . . . but it all happened so fast, Shuri can't remember any of it.

"The palace and grounds have been swept, top to bottom, four times over," a male voice crackles over the prehistoric intercom system. "There is no trace of the presence of any unauthorized persons."

"But there *was* someone here who should not have been, yes?" Mother asks.

"We believe so, Your Majesty," comes the reply. "The intruder was swift and seemed to know how to avoid being caught on film, but we were able to capture some small bits of footage—"

"But they got away is what you are saying."

There's a long pause during which Shuri wonders if the old communication device has finally failed. But then the voice responds, audibly defeated. "That is correct, my queen."

"So not only did someone get *into* this palace unhindered . . . they also managed to get out?"

Another pause, then: "That is correct, my queen."

"Unbelievable," Mother says.

"I can assure you that we will stay on top of them, Your Majesty," comes a voice Shuri recognizes: Ayo's. "I am certain General Okoye has already entered the fray. We Dora Milaje are respectful of security jurisdictions, but we are very much sworn to protect the throne and all members of the royal family. A threat on the palace is a threat on you, Shuri, and T'Challa, and we are not taking that lightly."

Mother doesn't respond, and a thick hush fills the bunker space.

After what feels like an eternity—but is likely only a few seconds—Shuri can't take the charged silence anymore. She swears if anyone moves, static electricity will shoot out like lightning and zap everyone unconscious. She slowly opens her eyes and lets out a sleepy groan.

Biiiiig stretch for effect.

"What time is it?" Shuri says through a dramatically fake yawn. "Where are we?"

"We are still in the bunker, Shuri," Mother says. "Which is most unfortunate."

"They are completing one final sweep of the grounds—" Nakia begins. But she gets cut short by the chiming of her Kimoyo bracelet. She lifts her forearm to eye level, and the upper half of Okoye appears above her wrist in hologram-form. "General," Nakia says.

"We are all clear, Nakia. Please escort the queen to the throne room, and have Ayo return the princess to her quarters—"

"I'd prefer to accompany Mother," Shuri says before she can catch herself.

"Unfortunately, Shuri, that is not a request we can accommodate at the moment," Okoye says. "I'm sure you are frightened and would prefer to stick close to your mother, but I can assure you that you will be well protected."

"But I'm not—" Shuri stops. *Frightened* is what she was going to say, but perhaps it's better to let the adults think what they'd like. In truth, the princess just wants to know what's going on. What happened. Why they've been in this outdated (and clearly Bast-forsaken) bunker for so long.

She knows, though, that expressing her curiosity would likely backfire with all the grown-ups so on edge. So she swallows it. There are certainly other means of getting the information she's after.

"Yes, General," she says with a nod.

"All right, then," Okoye replies. "I have dispatched additional Dora as well as a number of palace guards to supplement your ranks. They are waiting in the hallway."

The same palace guards who failed to keep an intruder out? Shuri wants to say but doesn't . . .

And it turns out, she doesn't need to.

"Let us pray to Bast that the gathered guards are

not the ones our intruder waltzed right past on his way in *and* out," Mother grumbles.

For a few moments, no one responds. It takes everything in the princess not to snort with laughter.

"Yes, Your Majesty," Okoye finally says. "Nakia, I will see you and the queen momentarily. Ayo, please join us once the princess is safe. There are already Dora posted outside her chambers, awaiting her return."

Which gives Shuri an idea . . . "Can K'Marah join me in my room? I would feel much better with her there."

"I'm afraid not, Princess," Okoye says. "For the time being, no one is permitted to enter or leave the palace grounds."

Drat. Shuri could've really used K'Marah's assistance. She lets her shoulders drop. "Yes, General," she says.

"Oh, and, Princess?" Okoye's voice takes on a sing-songy tone.

It catches Shuri off guard. "Hmm?" she replies, looking up.

Okoye's hologram has been turned so that the stern-looking general is facing Shuri. (In *this* moment, the princess deeply regrets adding the 360-degree rotational feature to the Kimoyo hologram-projection technology.) "No funny business, eh?" the general says. "This is a very serious matter, and we need unwavering compliance from you. Understand?"

"She absolutely does," Mother cuts in. And when Shuri sees the expression on her tired—yet undeniably *regal*—face, she *knows* that she'll see nothing beyond the walls of her quarters for the foreseeable future.

She gulps.

"Correct, Shuri?" Mother continues.

The princess nods so fervently, she's sure she looks like one of the bulbous, bouncy-headed toys T'Challa likes to collect of all his favorite American popular culture characters. "Yes, ma'am," Shuri says— vaguely fearing for her life. "I understand completely, General."

"Excellent," Okoye replies. "I bid you all adieu. And please: Be careful."

<hr/>

Shuri must admit: The journey back through the palace was . . . tense.

Not that anything *looked* different than when she'd last made the trip. It was more the presence of so many palace guards and Dora Milaje that put Shuri on edge—there are four of the former and six of the latter *just* for her.

(How utterly ironic.)

The Dora and guards do a full security sweep of the room and dressing chamber before the princess is permitted to enter. (Maybe shouldn't have left the dirty clothes from yesterday's sparring session with Kocha M'Shindi scattered across the floor . . .) And once she manages to convince Ayo that she does not, in fact, need a security detail *inside* the room, the uniformed cadre of overly stern adults finally exits, pulling the door shut behind them.

She creeps over to lock it. "Just in case!" she shouts through the thick, carved wood. "I feel a bit safer with it locked. Hope that's okay!"

The response is muffled but immediate: "Ah, Princess, we are not sure that is wise—"

"Going to take a nap now!" Shuri shouts, backing away. "Didn't sleep very well in that rigid bunker chair. Wake me if anything happens!"

After waiting ten seconds or so to make sure there's no further reply, Shuri turns on the balls of her socked feet and makes her way toward the dark doorway of her dressing chamber. Once inside, she takes one final peek over her shoulder at the entrance to her room, then quietly slides her in-room experimentation station out of its hidden slot in the wall.

When she first created the thing, she intended to use it solely for what its name implied: hypothesis-based experiments, most of which involved Vibranium. But during the monthlong *grounding* she had to endure as a result of sneaking out of the country (again), Shuri made a few upgrades to her closet laboratory. The most significant change was the addition of her latest invention: an ultra-slim touchscreen computer—with hologram projection capabilities—she'd connected to the palace's master server. And made completely untraceable.

It won't give the princess any sort of live access to conversations taking place in the throne room—*spying* through the use of listening devices contributed heavily to that monthlong grounding. But it *will* permit her to do some investigating of her own.

"All right, let's see what we've got," she whispers as the thing boots up. Once the home screen appears, she raises her voice slightly and says: "Hey, S.H.U.R.I., please pull up all palace security footage captured between eleven p.m. last night and seven a.m. this morning."

"As you wish, Your Majesty," the automated voice of her Super Heroics Universal Remote Interface blares into the air. Shuri scrambles to lower the volume before shutting her eyes and waiting to hear a knock on her door (surely the Dora heard that . . .).

No knock comes.

She exhales and watches the screen fill with thumb-nails of video footage. She knows there will be more than one hundred of them—one for each individual security camera in and around the palace.

After about one minute, the voice speaks again. "Command complete."

"Thank you," Shuri says. "Now please isolate all clips that experienced an anomaly during the stated time frame."

All but four disappear from the screen.

"Whoa," Shuri says, feeling something akin to real fear for the first time since she was plucked out of the spider dream. The palace security system is *surely* one of the best and most technologically advanced in the world. If the "intruder" truly managed to evade detection this thoroughly, they are a greater force to be reckoned with than she realized.

"S.H.U.R.I., please highlight the time stamps of the anomalies."

"Command complete," the voice says as a time frame appears beneath each of the remaining clips. The longest of the four lasts 1.2 seconds. All the others are half a second or shorter, and the time gap between the first anomaly and the final one is one minute twenty-eight seconds.

Shuri tries to gulp down the sense of dread that has

risen in her throat. She opens each clip in turn. Three of them are from the palace's exterior, and one of those three is useless: the flash of what appears to be an arm from one of the cameras at the main gate.

The other two exterior shots prove *slightly* more useful: Though the person is completely cloaked in black, it's clear that one flash is of the intruder entering the palace—through a door near the kitchens—and the other is of him exiting through the door that leads to the housekeeping staff quarters.

The fourth clip, though, is the one that makes Shuri suck in a breath. It's from *inside* the palace. In it, Shuri can see the intruder's heaving back—tall, but lankier than she would've expected—as he stands, staring at a section of smooth, bare wall. His head cocks left, then right.

"This is bad," she whispers, checking the location of this particular camera one final time. It confirms her suspicions.

The intruder—who got in *and* out of the palace in under two minutes—somehow managed to locate the hidden entrance to the Wakandan vault of relics.

3

HIGH ALERT

Sleep that night is a no-go.

Which isn't surprising in the least: Not only was Shuri confined to her quarters for the rest of the day—all necessities were delivered, and the Dora let her know she'd been excused from her classes—she was also kept completely in the dark (figuratively speaking). Not a single grown-up called or stopped by to give her any updates.

She forces herself into bed at around one a.m.— and left a light on—but when she closes her eyes, all she can see are the heaving shoulders (why was he breathing *so* hard?) of the person who crept into her home while she was sleeping, and got closer to her nation's most preciously guarded artifacts than anyone ever has.

In her lifetime, at least.

And no: The intruder didn't actually get *inside* the vault. In fact, Shuri can't *really* be sure that said intruder knew there was something beyond that particular section of wall.

But the fact remains: A stranger successfully infiltrated the most heavily guarded structure in all of Wakanda. It makes Shuri wonder how "secure" the palace actually is. If someone got in that easily once, what's to stop them from getting in again?

Another matter she's been trying *not* to think about (and miserably failing): The intruder zipped through the palace faster than Shuri knew possible. And *almost* without a trace. As much as she'd prefer to deny it, the princess knows this suggests familiarity with the layout of the grounds . . . and the palace itself.

What if the stranger is no stranger at all? What if the person who "broke in" is someone Shuri sees all the time?

From there, the princess's thoughts tumble down into a hole she has no idea how to get out of. Is there someone on the palace staff who would want to harm the royal family? How many people actually *know* about the vault of relics—and its contents?

What was that black-clad person *looking* for? Why didn't they actually take anything (that the princess knows of, at least)?

And when will they return? Because Shuri is absolutely certain that a return is imminent.

Once she does finally drift off to sleep—shortly after dawn, if the shifting light creeping through the curtains over her windows is any indication—Shuri is plagued by nightmares that combine her current quandary with her greatest fear: In one of these very much *not* lucid dreams—they feel all too real to the princess—a hairy black spider, with a body as long as T'Challa is tall, and thick, multi-jointed legs like a tarantula, crosses the royal grounds and begins to climb up the eastern wall of the palace. There's something white on its belly, but Shuri can't make it out from where she's peeking around the side of the building.

The spider reaches a window on the third floor, and Shuri gasps as its legs begin to retract into its body. Soon, instead of a giant arachnid clinging to the wall, there's a man. Cloaked in black from head to toe. He's wearing what appears to be a stretchy suit, similar in style to T'Challa's Vibranium-elastane Panther habit.

He opens the window and crawls inside, pulling it shut behind him.

And when Shuri blinks, she's somehow been transported to her bed. Which is inside her room . . . on the third floor.

The black-clad intruder is standing just beyond the foot of the bed. Staring at her. She thinks . . . She can't see his eyes. Or any facial features for that matter. Everything is blacked out.

"Where is it?" he says in a voice that's not nearly as deep as Shuri would've expected. (Though that doesn't make the encounter any less terrifying.) "I know you know," he continues. "Just tell me where it is." He takes a step closer.

Shuri opens her mouth to respond but is stopped by his creepily long limbs.

Were they like that before?

"It is *my* time now," he says, looming ever closer. Right before Shuri's eyes, four spider legs begin to grow out of the intruder's back. His arms morph, and for a moment he just stands there, part human, part big, ugly bug.

The princess can't breathe, let alone speak.

"Tell me!" he shouts, completing the transformation and climbing onto Shuri's bed.

With her heart beating faster than the djembe drum

roll used to announce T'Challa's arrival at a formal gathering, Shuri does what anyone with her level of combat and weapons training would do under these circumstances: She pulls the blanket over her head and squeezes her eyes shut.

She can feel the creature's weight shifting around on the mattress and hear pincers clicking right above her. Then, just as she knows it's about to strike, a deafening roar rings through the air, jolting her awake.

Shuri yells and startles so intensely, she gets tangled in the sheets, and flails herself right off the bed.

It's her alarm clock.

"Bast, that would be a *terrible* sound to wake to," comes a voice from the other side of the room. "Why would you torture yourself so, Shuri? Though I will admit: Setting an alarm for three-thirty in the afternoon is rather strange. Guess I shouldn't be surprised the alert is so wretched."

The princess has a vague memory of resetting the alarm in the middle of night but—

Wait.

She wiggles her head free from the twisted bedclothes and gasps. This time with delight.

"K'Marah!"

"Wow," Shuri's best friend—and partner in various

covert missions that have gotten them in quite a bit of trouble—said. "If I didn't know better, I would think you're happy to see me."

"I *am* happy to see you, K'Marah!"

The moment the words are out, Shuri realizes how true they are. The weight of the past couple of days drapes itself over her shoulders: from the phobia emersion therapy (she shudders at the thought) to being on lockdown for almost twenty-four hours without a single update.

And she hasn't been permitted to speak to anyone about any of it.

So now?

"You are like the sunrise that puts an end to the deepest, darkest night," Shuri says, so relieved she could cry. (Not that she *would*, though.) "I'm *thrilled* that you are here!"

K'Marah chuckles. "Well, tell me how you *really* feel, Princess."

"I'm serious! These past two days have been horrendous!"

At this, the Dora-in-training's eyes drop.

Which gives Shuri pause. "Wait . . . do you know what's going on?" she asks her friend. It wouldn't be the first time K'Marah is privy to information the princess doesn't have.

"Huh?"

"Around *here*. No one will tell me anything, and it's driving me mad. So if you have information, K'Marah—"

"I don't, I don't!" She raises her hands. "I swear it on—"

"Don't *swear* it on anything," Shuri says with a disappointed huff. "I believe you. How did you get in here, by the way?" The princess finally extricates herself from the twisted bedding and climbs to her feet. "I was told no one would be allowed in or out—" Which is when Shuri notices K'Marah's *'fit*, as the shorter girl likes to call her clothing ensembles.

And the princess's mouth falls open.

It makes K'Marah smile.

"K'Marah, are you—?"

"A Dora Karami now?" K'Marah jumps to her feet and looks down at her standard-issue red-brown-and-gold Dora Milaje uniform. "Yes! I am!"

Shuri's head cocks to one side, not wanting to kill her best friend's *vibe* or whatever but also needing to know . . . "Sure hope this doesn't reflect poorly on my princessing, but I don't think I've ever heard of that."

"Oh, that's the best part!" K'Marah practically squeals, bouncing on her toes. "The designation was created specifically for me!"

Shuri's eyebrows rise.

"It means *small and adored*, and is basically a promotion from Dora trainee to, like, a junior Dora Milaje. I'm the youngest person to ever be *allowed* to train, and Okoye made it clear that I'm not old enough to take the oath and assume full Dora duties. But she also said I was ready to level up. So Dora Karami it is. And *you* are my first official assignment!"

Assignment? "Huh?"

"Chop-chop, Princess," K'Marah says, drawing her back up completely straight and lifting her chin. "I have joined Ayo and Nakia as of one your personal guards. That being said, get dressed." She raises her arm and taps a Kimoyo bead. *15:37* illuminates in the air. "We have a small bit of leeway, but we are due at Upanga as near to sixteen hundred hours as possible."

<hr />

Call it intuition—the girls have been on a number of harrowing adventures together and can "read" each other fairly well—but there is zero doubt in Shuri's mind that her best friend has something *else* going on. Even beyond potentially being nervous about this first Dora Milaje Karami "assignment," the amount K'Marah is blinking, the tension evident in her shoulders, and her worrying at her lip with her teeth make it clear to Shuri that there's something the shorter girl isn't telling her.

They make it to Upanga with no incident and immediately step into sword strategy and spear-spinning drills. So it's not until the girls are awaiting their turn to spar that Shuri gets the chance to broach her suspicions. She leans into K'Marah and lowers her voice to a whisper. "You will develop a hole in your lip if you keep biting at it, Little Dora."

The other girl's face clouds over. And Shuri knows that K'Marah knows she's been caught. "Stop watching me so closely," the Dora hisses back. "It's creepy. And very unbecoming of a princess."

"Yeah, okay," Shuri replies. "What's going on, K'Marah?"

The first set of girls exits the mat, and the pair in front of Shuri and K'Marah step on. The princess and her Dora are next in line.

"I don't know what you're talking about," K'Marah says, sticking her nose into the air.

"Oh, you most certainly do," Shuri replies. "And you're going to tell me. I know you well enough to know that you won't be able to keep it in now."

K'Marah just scowls.

"You *do* know something about the palace break-in, don't you?"

At this, K'Marah looks at Shuri. And she is definitely offended. And looks ready to punch the princess (which she will certainly have the opportunity to do momentarily). "Did I not almost swear on the blessed heart of Bast that I *don't* know anything about that?"

"Okay, okay!" Shuri says, taking a tiny step back. "Don't get your braids in a knot. I can just tell something's off with you—"

"Princess Shuri and K'Marah!" a senior trainer calls out from across the mat. "You're up next! I would advise you to cease chattering and prepare yourselves."

"Yes, madam," K'Marah replies with a deferent bow of her head. Then through gritted teeth to Shuri: "Will you *drop* it? You're going to get us both in trouble."

The taller girl in the current match manages to get beneath the shorter one and flip her onto her back. She almost gets her pinned for the win, but the shorter girl kicks out of it at the last second. Buying Shuri a *little* more time.

"Just tell me what it is, and we can discuss later," the princess says. "We both know you are going to fight poorly if you try to hold it in . . ."

K'Marah's jaw clenches, but Shuri watches her relent. "Fine," she says. "I received—"

But she doesn't get to say any more. Because at that moment, a siren-style alarm blares.

The citywide security alert.

"He's back," Shuri says under her breath.

Then everything whips into chaos.

4

UNEXPECTED VISITOR

Despite grabbing weapons—the Dora Milaje–preferred Vibranium-tipped tetela lance for K'Marah, and a curved mambele sword for Shuri—and charging out with the other Dora, the two girls don't get very far.

"Shuri! K'Marah!" Ayo says the moment they make it through the exit. (She'd definitely been waiting.) "There you are! Put those weapons down, and you two come with me."

"Put them *down*?" K'Marah says, clearly confused. "But, Ayo—"

"You heard me correctly," the elder Dora replies. "We must hurry."

Thus, K'Marah's first assignment shifts: from Member of the Princess's Royal Guard to Person Who Must Stay By Her Side No Matter What. Which means that instead of finding out what's going on, and running into the fray to employ the training they've undergone—for such a time as this, no less—the princess and her junior Dora best friend are shoved into a hoverjet and whisked away to the Makao, a royal "safe house" Shuri didn't know existed.

It's quite annoying.

"Well, this is rich," K'Marah grumbles once they're in the air, voicing precisely what Shuri is thinking. "So much for that Dora Karami thing." She looks over at Shuri, wide-eyed. "I mean . . . no offense, of course, Your Majesty—"

"Oh, cut it out," Shuri says with a wave. "I'm just as frustrated as you are. And don't get all weird now that hanging out with me is technically your *job*."

At this, the princess gazes out at the buildings and trees zipping by beneath them, and a knot forms in her throat. Soon there's something *wet* running down her face.

"Oh, Shuri!" K'Marah says, throwing her arms

around her friend far more dramatically than warranted. "Everything will be okay!"

To Shuri's shock, this burst of tenderness from her friend cracks something inside her. Now she *really* starts crying. (And thanking Bast for the soundproof partition between the small passenger cabin where she and K'Marah are seated and the cockpit space hosting Ayo and their pilot.)

"Someone snuck into the palace two nights ago," the princess says. "While everyone was sleeping."

K'Marah doesn't respond, so Shuri surges forward.

"And no one will tell me anything. I just keep getting shushed. *'Not now, Shuri.' 'This isn't the time, Shuri.' 'Stay in your room, Shuri.'*" As she talks, Shuri's despair morphs to anger. "I'm first in line to the throne! And *I* know that the intruder was trying to get into the vault of relics—"

"You know that *how*, exactly?"

"Oh . . ." Should she tell the truth? Might as well . . . "I accessed the security footage captured during the 'home invasion,' as they say in America. And let me tell you: The rhetoric is accurate."

"Got it," K'Marah says. "You were saying?"

"It just seems so . . . unfair."

"And a bit cruel, if you ask me," K'Marah replies.

"Cruel?"

"Absolutely. If your mother and brother know you as well as *I* do—and I would hope that's the case—they would know that keeping *this* kind of information from you basically amounts to cruel and usual punishment. You practically fall to pieces when you *don't* know something—"

"Oh, shut up." But Shuri smiles and wipes her face. "And here I thought you were going to say something of *merit*."

"Whatever, Princess. You're only mad because it's true."

The girls lapse into silence, both a bit more relaxed now. They are crossing over the baobab plain and passing the Sacred Mound. Shuri sighs a circle of fog on the window, wishing above all else that she and K'Marah could just go to her lab.

"So, ummm . . . where exactly *is* this 'Makao' thing we're being whisked off to?" K'Marah asks.

"Your guess is as good as mine. We could be headed to that base in London for all I know. Clearly nobody tells *me* anything these days."

"Henny reached out to me," K'Marah blurts, seemingly out of nowhere.

The words take a few moments to register in Shuri's brain—there's more jostling around in there for her attention than usual. But once they do? Her head whips right so fast, it's a wonder it doesn't fly from her shoulders.

"Say *what*?"

"I was trying to tell you at Upanga. But then the siren sounded and we got rushed out. He sent me a message—"

But that's all she gets out. Because there's a crackle of static before a voice comes over the intercom: "Prepare for landing, ladies. We have reached our destination."

◈◈◈◈

The princess outright *refuses* to exit the hoverjet.

"No way," she says, shaking her head. "I am *not* going in there."

"Oh, where's your sense of adventure, Princess?" K'Marah asks, face alight with excitement.

In front of them looms a structure Shuri's only been to once. And it was for a thing she's not very keen on being forced to remember: Baba's burial.

"Nope," she asserts again, staring up at the Necropolis. Wakanda's city of the dead, and the final resting place of every person to carry the mantle of Black Panther. "Not happening."

Multiple hundred-foot-tall stone slabs jut out of the ground at an angle—almost like the wind tried to blow them over but gave up. In fact, seeing the telltale

Stonehenge-style slanted boulders, which are shaped like spearheads, reminds Shuri of the question that would always pop up anytime she thought of the mysterious burial grounds: *Where* had the stones comes from, and how had they been erected?

She's almost tempted to ask . . . but then remembers that the adults want her and K'Marah to go *in* there.

Wherever *in there* actually is. She certainly doesn't see a building.

"Shuri—" K'Marah begins. But the princess cuts her off.

"Nope." She crosses her arms. "No way."

"You will be safe here, Your Majesty," Ayo says. "There is a space specifically *designed* for such a time as—"

"Such a time as *what*, Ayo?" says Shuri, frustration boiling over. "K'Marah and I don't even know what's going on!"

At this, Ayo sighs and rests her hands on the princess's shoulders, then locks her in a gaze Shuri can't seem to break. "I know this is a lot to take in, Shuri. But unprecedented times call for unprecedented measures," the Dora says. "The *moment* we have a handle on the situation, I will tell you everything you'd like to know. You have my word. For now, you and K'Marah will be safe here—"

"Wait, you're *leaving*?" K'Marah cuts in.

"Not for long," Ayo replies. "I am needed in the city, but I shall return for you both as soon as possible. As I mentioned, the safe house here was *made* for a situation like this one. You have to trust me."

Shuri exhales and lets her chin drop. Accepting defeat. "All right," she says, not feeling all right at all, but not seeing any other options. "Lead the way, I guess," she says to Ayo.

The other woman nods and turns to head toward the stones.

◇◇◇◇

To both Shuri's and K'Marah's shock, the Makao is small but well appointed.

The entrance is tucked beneath the second-tallest slanted boulder—and thankfully a comfortable distance away from the Panther mausoleum—and after a descent down a short set of stairs and walk up a cave-like hallway (not unlike the one that leads to Shuri's lab), the girls are led into what amounts to a small apartment. There's a tiny living area with a state-of-the-art curved-screen television; a completely stocked kitchen; a bedroom with two large, pillow-covered beds; and a full washroom, fluffy linens included.

As soon as Ayo leaves and they hear the dead bolt

on the massive steel door click into place, Shuri drops down onto the small sofa. "Well, this is certainly better than the palace bunker," she says.

"Don't think I realized the palace *had* a bunker. Though now that you've said it, of course it does." K'Marah unhooks her silver neck cuff and removes the titanium plates from her shoulders and forearms. She lets the implements fall to the floor and then plops down beside the princess. "Bast, those things are uncomfortable," she says—then immediately claps her hands over her mouth.

"Ahh . . . are you all right?" Shuri asks.

K'Marah lowers her voice to a whisper. "I don't think I'm supposed to say that."

At this, Shuri laughs.

"What's so funny??" K'Marah balks.

But Shuri can't *stop* laughing now. All of it is so utterly ridiculous. From some black-clad creep getting into the most fortified building in the nation, to her and her (semi) *official* Dora Milaje best friend being trapped in a fancy underground cave within Wakanda's most sacred cemetery. Completely in the dark as to *why*.

"How absurd it all is, K'Marah," she says. Then she slides down into the couch and shuts her eyes. The past few days and lack of sleep settle over her, practically pressing her down into the cushions. "Go on with your story."

"My story?"

"Yes. About the message you received and failed to immediately share with me." Shuri yawns. "You know: from the boy who almost wiped out the heart-shaped herb."

"Shuri—"

"What did it say, K'Marah?"

But whether or not K'Marah answers, Shuri doesn't know. While K'Marah continues to ramble on, she's out like a light.

Shuri . . .

The voice that filters into Shuri's mind is quiet but insistent.

Shuri! You have to wake up . . .

Then comes a sense of pressure around her forearm. It gets tighter . . .

Shuri, wake UP, please . . .

Tighter . . .

SHURI!

"Oww!" Shuri snatches her arm away from K'Marah, fully awake now . . .

And immediately freezes.

"What is it, Shuri?" K'Marah whispers.

But Shuri can't speak. Because there, in front of the girls—*inside* their "safe house," the door of which is standing open—is a person cloaked in a stretchy suit like T'Challa's Panther habit, but all black.

Just like in Shuri's dream.

Unlike the person in Shuri's dream, however, this . . . *creature* (or is it the creature's suit?) has a face: Large, white crescent-shaped eyes sit above an oversize mouth . . . full of row upon row of horrifyingly sharp teeth.

Its shoulders heave just as they did in the short security clip.

"I'm dreaming," Shuri says. "Must be. What time is it? This is a dream, yes?"

"It's"—K'Marah taps a Kimoyo bead to check the time—"two seventeen. In the morning. And no . . ." she says. "Not a dream."

"It has to be. Because we're in the Makao, or whatever it's called, aren't we? A *safe* house? Where no one—or no . . . thing—can find us?"

"We are clearly very much *found*, Shuri," K'Marah says. Then . . .

"OWW!" from the princess. "Why are you pinching me, K'Marah?"

"See? Totally real. You felt that pinch. What do we do?"

Panic expands in Shuri's throat, making it impossible for her to speak.

"Shuri?"

The creature takes a step toward them.

Both girls scream—

And it takes a step back and crouches down, slapping its hands over where ears would be on a normal human head.

Which gives Shuri pause. "Sensitivity to sound?" she says, now more curious than afraid.

"Not sure . . ." K'Marah replies. "Should we scream again?"

"No," the princess says. Because something occurs to her: The girls are still very much *alive*. She'd been *sleeping*, for Bast's sake. Easy prey. And K'Marah clearly wasn't posing any threat. "I don't think it wants to hurt us," she deduces.

"*WE*," comes a voice that sounds like it's been gargling gravel (definitely *not* like in her dream).

"Huh?" from Shuri.

"*WE*," the creature repeats.

"Are you going to eat us?" K'Marah blurts.

Shuri jabs her friend with an elbow. "K'Marah! Rude!"

"We kind of need to know, don't we?"

"We just want gem," the scary spider guy cuts in.

"Who is *we*?" K'Marah says as Shuri says, "What gem?"

He looks back and forth between them as if trying to decide who to answer.

Shuri squeezes K'Marah's hand. "We're sorry, Mr. . . . what was your name?"

"Name . . . not important," he says. "Need gem."

"Forgive my ignorance, but . . . what gem, exactly?"

"Nebular gem," he replies.

Nebular gem? Shuri's never heard of such a thing. Could that be in the vault of relics? "Do you . . . know where it is?" she asks.

"You have," he says, pointing right at her.

"Uhhhh . . ."

"Whatever it is, just give it to him," K'Marah says. "We have far too much promise to be eaten by a monster—"

"WE NOT MONSTER!" he yells, stepping forward.

"Okay, okay!" from K'Marah.

"Can it, Little Dora!" Shuri says through clenched teeth. Then she takes a deep breath, knowing that what she's about to say is true, but also knowing this nameless person (creature?) probably isn't going to like it.

Lying, however, doesn't feel like the right thing to do.

"I'm sorry." She manages to shove past the expanding knot in her throat. "I truly don't have what you're looking for."

At first, he doesn't respond, just stares at Shuri like he's gauging whether or not she's telling the truth.

Then he steps back and nods.

"Princess no have on person . . . We will find."

And he bounds out the open door into the darkness beyond.

MISSION LOG

THERE IS A HIGH PROBABILITY THAT WE WILL REGRET IT, BUT WHEN AYO RETURNED FOR K'MARAH AND ME—NOT UNTIL THE NEXT MORNING, MIND YOU—WE MADE NO MENTION OF OUR SPECIAL VISITOR.

This is not a decision my Dora Karami and I came to lightly, but after one hour and thirty-four minutes of debrief followed by four hours of fitful sleep in what were surprisingly comfortable beds—we decided it was the wisest choice. For one, it is as clear as acetic acid that despite our saving the nation, rescuing a cadre of girl geniuses from certain doom, AND creating the invisible dome that will keep our country safe from unwanted visitors (this one excluded, obviously), the adults still don't trust that my Dora Karami and I can handle this sort of thing. Also apparent: He is far too much for THEM to handle—he managed to get to US while everyone in the capital was looking for HIM.

Once back inside the hoverjet, Ayo gave us a quick rundown of what was going on. "At the request of your brother," she said (thank Bast SOMEONE finally recognized my need to know these things as a member of the royal family). Of course, some of it I already knew from my sleuthing . . . but here's a full recap of what she said.

- Two nights ago, an intruder managed to subvert all security measures and access the palace. (Aware of this, obviously.)
- He avoided tripping any alarms until he reached a hallway where he paused for a second too long. (Was not aware of the alarm bit; did know about the pause.)

- Said alarm seemed to trigger some sort of reaction for the intruder; one guard said that when he spotted him, it looked as though said intruder was "attempting to remove his own head from his shoulders with his hands." (His reaction to K'Marah's and my "teenybopper banshee screeches," as T'Challa once put it, aligns with this.)

- Another handful of eyewitnesses on the grounds—mostly palace staff— claim he was "possessed of speed and strength that rivals our own Black Panther's." (Not sure about THAT, but certainly not completely implausible.)

- The guards and Dora Milaje have yet to figure out what he was looking for inside the palace (how bizarre that I know something they don't), or where he went after he left . . .

- And today, he entered the Golden City and stormed two locations: the observatory and the Sayansi Museum of Wakandan History; it is said that at the latter, he went straight to the Hall of Celestial Artifacts, and left from there through a window. (Certainly in line with the name of the thing he asked *me* for.)

- He has again vanished without a trace. He was (allegedly) last spotted in the city by a night watchman at 01:31. (Approximately forty-six minutes before arriving at the Makao safe house, which is thirty-seven kilometers from the city center. If these times are correct, it would mean our strange humanoid pal can run 74.59 kilometers, or forty-six miles, per hour.)
- (Perhaps he IS faster than T'Challa!)

While K'Marah and I haven't figured out precisely what to DO yet, we both feel that taking the next twenty-four hours to see what we can find out about our visitor—and this "nebular gem" bounty he is after—would be a good idea. THEN we can tell the grown-ups about him AND give some useful information.

There were roughly thirty-nine hours between the intruder's trip through the palace and his visits to the observatory and museum. Let's hope he maintains a similar pattern.

That will give us the twenty-four hours we need.

5

READY

They don't get twenty-four hours.

In fact, when the palace alarm blares that evening at eleven p.m., Shuri is still awake, sifting through the Internet for information about this *nebular gem*.

When Ayo and Nakia burst into her room, Shuri is standing in her pajamas and bathrobe, ready to be whisked to the bunker. With slippers on this time, and her Kimoyo card in her pocket. (Sure hope there's a decent Wi-Fi signal in that den of technological antiquity.)

For a moment, they both just stand there, clearly shocked that Shuri is so . . . up and at 'em. "You're awake," Nakia says.

Mastress of the obvious, that one.

"I don't think anyone could sleep *through* that alarm," Shuri says, hoping against hope that neither woman will remember that she *did*, in fact, sleep through this exact same alarm a mere three nights ago. Mother had shaken her awake. "Are we going?" Shuri continues before either of them can respond.

"Oh, yes, yes!" Ayo says, snapping back to attention. "We are. Let's go."

The senior Dora Milaje lead the princess on a different route to the bunker—this time through a passageway accessed by a secret door in the royal coat closet—and when they arrive, Shuri is shocked (if not slightly relieved) that the queen isn't there.

"Ahh . . . where is Mother?" she asks. Which triggers a different question: Has her kingly brother returned? "And T'Challa?"

Nakia and Ayo look at each other, and then Nakia sighs. "T'Challa is still on his mission."

"Wait. Are you *kidding*—"

Nakia puts a hand up. "We know nothing about it, Princess. Only that he spoke with your mother."

"And speaking of the queen: She decided she'd be

more useful down in the security center," Ayo follows.

"So *I* am the only person who has to hole up in this Bast-awful bunker?"

Ayo shrugs. "We're sorry, Your Majesty. Orders were given, and we took an oath to follow them."

"On the bright side, though . . ." Nakia begins as she pulls the door shut and locks it tight. "We have entertainment!" She reaches beneath the central sash that reaches from her collarbone to her knees. (Shuri has always wondered why the thing is there. It seems so impractical for a group of warriors who have to shift and move quickly.) Then holds up a small red box.

"*Uno?*" Shuri says, reading the word printed on said box aloud. "Doesn't that mean *one* in Spanish?"

"Precisely!" Nakia replies. Shuri's not sure she's ever seen her so outwardly excited. "It's an American card game where you match colors and/or numbers, and once you have only one card left, you shout '*UNO!*'"

Neither Shuri nor Ayo says anything.

"I will teach you both how to play," Nakia continues, striding across the room to take a seat at the far end of the long table. Shuri's guessing she'll be required to sit at the head again.

She sighs.

"Come, come, come," Nakia says. "There is no telling how long we will be in here, so we might as well make the most of it, yes?"

Shuri hates to be the bubble burster, but she has work to do. "Ah . . . not to steal your sunshine, Nakia, but I have some tasks I need to complete on my—"

"Kimoyo card," Ayo says, rolling her eyes. "Fine, fine," and she waves Shuri off. (Not that there's anywhere for the princess to go.) "Young people," she says to Nakia as she takes the seat across from her. "So addicted to their *technology* and *devices*. Teach *me* to play, Nakia."

And just like that, Shuri is free to . . . well, sit and look at her Kimoyo card. Though she won't be on PantherTube—which she's *sure* the Dora women are assuming. Because as soon as she was back in her quarters post-encounter with the nameless intruder—whom she's guessing has already left the palace like he did last time—she wiped a bunch of unnecessary stuff from the Kimoyo card's memory and pulled together an "app," as she's heard T'Challa say, that gives her full access to the palace's security camera network.

She removes her specially designed earbuds from the pocket of her robe and holds them up so Ayo and Nakia can see them. "Okay?" she asks the two women.

"Fine by us," Nakia says. Then she turns back to

Ayo. "Now, *this* is a draw-four wild card, and the most powerful card in the deck—"

Shuri pops the small hearing device into her ears, and the world goes silent.

She smiles. A short time ago, she upgraded the noise-cancellation mechanism in the admittedly store-bought earbuds by adding a tiny ring of Vibranium to the interior. So now nothing at all can get into her ears unless she wants it there.

And she wants nothing distracting her from the security footage.

As Shuri suspects, there's very little to actually see. Five images come up this time, three of them with his full body in the frame for at least one full second. (*Getting sloppy, are we?* the princess thinks but doesn't say.) She knows he's gone again because the last clip—which is 1.3 seconds long—is from the camera at the loading dock. He appears, looks around, and then runs off into the night.

Also of note: He does *not* go to the hallway where the entrance to the vault of relics is hidden within the wall. Which the princess finds very interesting. What was the purpose of entering the palace *this* time if it wasn't to try and get in there?

The irony hits her then: She is sitting in a maximum-security, atomic bomb–proof bunker to keep her "safe" from a being she's not only seen up close but has conversed with. And she knows precisely what he's looking for.

When the security footage proves useless, Shuri taps over to her web browser to look up this *nebular gem* the intruder is after. While there isn't much *public* on the gem itself, she does come across a password-protected and encrypted website that is intensely sketchy but may be her only chance at a true lead.

Within three seconds, she's managed to hack into it. "Flimsy American cybersecurity," she whispers under her breath.

Her breath that catches once she sees what's on the site. It appears to belong to a group of people who call themselves The Collectors, who buy, sell, and trade objects like nothing Shuri has ever seen. There's a stone that's said to give the possessor power over all space, near and far. There's a golden horn shaped like an elephant's tusk that was allegedly used by a god-king who reigned over what is now the American state of Georgia; he left behind chunks of the glistening metal when he vanished from Earth, never to be seen again. A rusted bronze spear that is said to have been used to slay a literal Titan (definitely the ugliest offering there . . . but oddly not the tallest tale). And a prismatic carved swan that was said to have its origins in something called the Bifrost on a planet called Asgard.

Shuri doesn't find anything about a nebular gem on the "For Sale or Comparable Trade" page, but she does find something she's not expecting: an image of a small glass case housing a dice-size block of an odd-looking metal. *Antarctic Vibranium*, according to the person who made the listing. Its description contains a warning: *Keep away from all other metals, as proximity to Antarctic Vibranium will liquefy them instantly. Wakandan Vibranium included.*

And though seeing the name of her country on this strange site gives Shuri a chill, she forges ahead and taps the link that will take her to the "Recently Sold and/or Comparably Traded" page.

"HA!" she shouts as she locates the listing for a *nebular gem* halfway down.

She happens to look up then and sees both Ayo and Nakia staring at her in alarm. "Is . . . everything okay?" Shuri asks, removing one of her earbuds.

"You tell us, Princess," Ayo remarks. "You're the one shouting."

"Oh. Sorry." Whoops! "Just watching this video about a . . . kid on laughing gas after leaving the dentist. It's quite funny!"

"Yeah, okay," Nakia says. (Clearly still peeved

about Shuri not wanting to play Uno.) She turns back to Ayo. "Your turn, sis."

The princess exhales and returns to her sleuthing. According to the listing, the nebular gem is "*a celestial artifact, forged during the creation of a planet known only as Battleworld; it gives whoever wields it the ability to move through space-time by means of molecular disintegration and regeneration.*"

Shuri shakes her head and rereads.

Disintegration and *regeneration*? So, like . . . the wielder of the gem would come apart and then reform somewhere else?

Sounds like absolute *upuuzi*.

(Nonsense.)

She continues reading.

The gem was allegedly acquired by some American arms dealer (though how it wound up on Earth is missing from the description) who, after accidentally sending himself to "*a planet full of rock giants*," returned home and sold it on the "*Black Market.*" Whatever that is.

It then passed through five or six other pairs of hands before one of the collectors got hold of it. He then traded it to a different collector . . .

Named Zanda. The princess of Narobia.

"No way," Shuri whispers.

She lowers her Kimoyo card then.

Her sole encounter with Zanda involved the near annihilation of the heart-shaped herb and almost invasion of Wakanda—on a Challenge Day, no less. Shuri's fists clench at the audacity of the Narobian woman. She and K'Marah stopped the multi-point assault *and* saved the herb almost single-handedly. (They'd had some help from Shuri's surrogate big sis, Queen Ororo of Kenya—or Ms. X-Woman Lady Storm, as K'Marah refers to her. But still.)

What's occurring to Shuri now, though: She doesn't actually know what *happened* to Princess Zanda. Shuri was *told* that Zanda was returned to her home country within a tube that contained a tornado whipping around her inside it, but whether or not she ever got *out*, the Wakandan princess isn't sure.

Something else Shuri doesn't know but would like to: If Zanda is the last-known person in possession of this *nebular gem*, why is the intruder poking around in Wakanda instead of Narobia? Does he somehow know that Zanda was here?

Which begs a different question: Who/what *is* this intruder, and how does he know of Wakanda's existence?

Shuri raises her Kimoyo card again and begins a new virtual hunt, tapping *"black-suited creature with razor-sharp teeth"* into the search bar. (Why people her age prefer this thumb *tap-tap-tapp*ing at letters on a screen as their primary form of communication is beyond the princess. The tedium would drive her mad.)

To her utter shock, that precise phrase returns 217,000 results (in 0.21 seconds, no less).

The first page is useless—filled with bizarre Halloween costumes and talk of extraterrestrials. But at the top of page two? She finds all she needs to see. Because she recognizes the organization mentioned in the article (which admittedly is housed on a website very clearly dedicated to conspiracy theorizing).

S.H.I.E.L.D.

Time to make a call to U.S. Colonel Nicholas Joseph Fury.

6
INTEL

The moment Shuri steps back into her quarters some three hours later, she knows something's off. (Though, fine: Playing Uno did make the time pass more quickly.)

She also knows that Ayo and Nakia are going to sweep the room before allowing her to enter . . . But she hopes to Bast that they don't find anything—or anyone. Shuri would like to examine the area for herself.

As the Dora move through Shuri's space, their spears at the ready, the princess makes a big show of being *extra* exhausted. "I mean you lovely ladies no disrespect"—big yawn and stretch for effect—"but if we could speed things up *just* a smidge . . . I am quite tired and would like to go to bed now. It is almost three a.m. after all."

"Duly noted, Your Majesty," Ayo replies with a reverent bow of her head. Shuri still hasn't gotten used to that. "We will check your dressing chambers, and then I will post just outside the door. Nakia will stay in here with—"

"NO!" Shuri shouts before she can catch herself.

Ayo pulls back in alarm.

"Sorry, sorry," Shuri says. "It's just that . . . I don't know that I'd be able to sleep with someone *inside* my quarters. Well . . . besides K'Marah." She's on the verge of rambling now. "But I've been sharing sleeping spaces with K'Marah for *years*, you see, so it's very different—"

"All right, all right," Nakia says, lifting hands in surrender. "We will both stay outside. But if you change your mind once you shut off the light and the dark settles, just shout and one of us will come in. Yes, we received the all clear from palace security, but I know how jolting these situations can be."

"Correct," Ayo chimes in. "So we are here for you. Another Dora will relieve me in one hour, but Nakia will be here until morning. Okay?"

Shuri nods. "Okay!" *Yikes, too exuberant...* "Umm ... thank you both very much. For ... protecting me and all that. Good night!"

She gives a little wave and turns to walk to her bed. Within a few seconds, she hears the door click shut behind her.

Which is when she jumps into her *own* high alert.

Someone was inside her quarters while she was not. She knows this to be fact as certainly as she knows every property of Wakandan Vibranium. She can *feel* it.

She hasn't shut off the light, so she's able to see the entire space clearly. Nothing *looks* out of place. But there's something almost tangible in the air. The ... ghost, for lack of a better term, of someone's (or something's?) presence.

She turns in a circle, taking the room in. Everything is precisely the way she left it and completely undisturbed—which, believe it or not, is easier for her to see when there's a bit of a mess—but it clicks: The curtain that typically covers the entrance to her dressing chamber was open even before Nakia stepped a foot toward it.

Shuri always leaves it closed.

Her eyes go wide then. Because if someone was in

there, it could spell Very Bad News. Especially if that someone was a black-suited, human-shaped, spider-ish creature person: She keeps a stash of Vibranium *and* weapons hidden inside.

No, none of the weapons are lethal: a few updated kitty cannon blasters that shoot electromagnetic energy, a pair of light gauntlets, a long-range stun gun . . . But in the wrong hands, they could certainly all render palace guards and/or Dora Milaje unconscious long enough to get past them. In fact, the stun gun shock is so intense that for a few minutes after coming to, the victim of one of those discharges is so disoriented, an enemy could get them to divulge just about any bit of information said enemy was after.

And there's no telling what a non-Wakandan would do with the stash of Vibranium.

Shuri carefully approaches, her Kimoyo card in hand. If nothing else, she'll be able to temporarily blind *any* intruder with the flashlight long enough to knock him (or her . . . or them . . .) to the floor. She thinks.

She sloooooowly peeks around the curtained side of the doorway . . . and finds her stash-away lab center partially pulled out. *Shuri* certainly didn't leave it that way—she always makes sure to slide everything back in place and seal it up tight. Yes, Mother knows there's a miniature laboratory in Shuri's closet, but she doesn't know how to get into it if it's shut.

The closer Shuri gets to the scene of who-knows-what-she'll-find, the louder her heartbeat thrums in her ears. (Too bad noise-canceling earbuds can't cancel *that*.) And once she has the station completely pulled out, she stumbles backward in surprise. And not because anything's missing . . .

All the things she keeps hidden—from the jars of various chemical concoctions, to the hunks of raw Vibranium, to the weapons—are knocked over and moved around.

Shuri begins to go through every jar and container she had stashed. Someone—nameless, black-clad, smile-of-death being, if she had to guess—went through them.

All of them, Shuri realizes. Every single last one.

But it doesn't look like anything was taken.

We just want gem rings that croaky voice in her head.

He was clearly telling the truth . . .

But why is he so convinced that *Shuri* has it?

◈◈◈◈

The next day, Shuri is permitted to go to her lab.

Surrounded by more guards than she's ever seen in one place at one time.

In an armored, tank-shaped hovercraft. (Perhaps

her nation *is* well equipped to handle an invasion of enemy forces.)

That's a part of a fleet of similar vehicles.

Thankfully, her best friend is with her. "Ahh . . . this is a bit *overkill*, don't you think?" K'Marah whispers from her five-point-harnessed position in the seat beside Shuri's. ("What are we, toddlers?" she'd said quite *loudly* as a pair of stoic and silent male guards strapped them both in.)

"Definitely overkill," Shuri replies. Then she leans closer to her friend. "Especially since we already know what we're dealing with here. Sort of."

"Was he really in your *room*?"

"*Shhhhhh!*" the princess hisses. "No one knows that but you. And I'd like to keep it that way."

"Valid." K'Marah nods and drags her finger and thumb across her lips in a zipping motion.

(The drama with that one.)

They ride in silence the remainder of the half-hour journey—moving in fleet-mode slows things down a bit. But the second the outer door to the lab seals itself shut—with all the security personnel *outside* it—Shuri launches into go-mode.

"Okay, so this is the information I was able to gather since we last saw each other." She tells K'Marah everything she learned about the elusive nebular gem, and how Zanda was the last person known to have it. ("Too bad that tall troll of a woman didn't accidentally disintegrate herself and 'regenerate' right into that churning red storm on the surface of Jupiter" was K'Marah's reply to that part.)

And then they get to the intruder. "I only read one article," Shuri admits. "But I felt like that was all I needed to read."

"Uhhh . . . why?"

They step into the center lab station, the home of Shuri's trusty desktop computer (which she basically rebuilds every few months to keep it current). The princess boots the machine up and the monitor comes to life. "Because it mentions S.H.I.E.L.D."

◈◈◈◈◈

Within forty-five minutes, the girls are collapsing on the couch in the lab's central atrium.

"Talk about information overload," K'Marah says.

Shuri's reply is uncharacteristically succinct: "Tell me about it."

Fury, surprisingly, answered on their first attempted call. Which caught both girls off guard—they usually have to call multiple times over the course of multiple hours to get hold of him. But then Shuri remembers one key fact: Her beloved big bro is on a mission with the shiny-headed man.

"Got a little free time today," he said when he picked up. (*Must not be* that *intense of a mission*, the princess thinks.)

And free time he certainly *did* have. Enough, in fact, to not only tell the girls about his encounters with an "individual" he called Venom ("Not always pretty") but also to explain precisely what Venom is: an extra-terrestrial symbiote.

"Based on your description of this 'strange visitor,' as you put it, my guess is he's one of the Klyntar," Fury says. He then treats the Wakandan princess and her best friend to a rundown of the alien's abilities and a full, extensive history of the symbiote's kind.

Fury did ask how the symbiote managed to get *into* Wakanda—and seemed a little jealous. (Shuri, of course, didn't have an answer, though she's certainly determined to get one. She definitely *didn't* tell him the intruder managed to break into the Wakandan palace. Twice.)

This is how Fury got into talking about how "the Venom symbiote," as he kept referring to the version he was familiar with, made its way to Earth: "It's a long story, but the gist is that a group of U.S. Super Heroes was transported against their will to some far-off planet we know only as 'Battleworld'—"

"Wait," Shuri said, recalling that name. "You . . .

wouldn't happen to know anything about something called the nebular gem, would you?"

"Can't say I do, kid."

Shuri rolled her eyes. She hated when he called her *kid*. So condescending. "Go on," she said.

"Well, Spider-Man—"

("I've seen him on PantherTube!" K'Marah interjected in the loudest whisper Shuri thinks she's ever heard.)

Fury laughs. "Well, his suit got completely destroyed in a fight on Battleworld, and a symbiote wound up bonding to him in the form of a *new* suit. Then good ol' Spidey came back to Earth with it."

The girls learned that Spider-Man eventually rejected the sentient alien suit, and it found and bonded with a different guy. And then another and another and another.

Which is how he landed at the question that put both girls' brains at full capacity: "So who is this one's host?"

"Host?" Shuri replied.

"Yeah. The symbiotes are useless on their own. They gotta bond with someone. Usually someone it feels like it can relate to. Then it takes on that someone's persona. Feels what the person is feeling and exacerbates it. Sifts through the person's hopes and dreams, and becomes personally invested in them—"

Shuri didn't hear much more after that. She was too struck. She vaguely hears something about Fury having an "idea" he would run by T'Challa to "get you Wakandans some assistance" before he ended the call, but her head was spinning. If the intruder really is this symbiote thing Fury is talking about, and it has taken on the "hopes and dreams" of what must be a Wakandan host (how else would it know its way around?), and it has broken into the palace twice—

"*They* really are a person," K'Marah says out of the blue. "Like, partially, at least, right? Fury said these things have to have a someone to attach themselves to . . ."

"Yeah" is all Shuri can muster.

Because one thing is abundantly clear: She not only has to find out how the symbiote got in, but also which Wakandan is "hosting" it. And why.

7

LURE

Shuri has no idea if this is going to work.

"Is this going to work?" K'Marah asks from her crouch position beside the princess.

"I don't know, K'Marah!" Shuri huffs. "For Bast's sake, you must stop asking me these unanswerable questions. You are going to drive me mad!"

"Fine. Sheesh."

The girls are on the ridge of a short cliff near the Sacred Mound. Which is both blessing and curse: There are so many guards stationed *around* the mound, Shuri and K'Marah have permission to roam the area without a squadron of Dora on top of them. (Also helpful: K'Marah was able to flex her Dora Milaje Karami status when Ayo attempted to object to the girls "going for a walk within the guarded area.")

However, despite them being alone—and having a bit of space to enact Shuri's plan—the area *is* truly full of guards. And while the presence of guards certainly hasn't stopped their symbiote—because after a bit more research, Shuri is certain that is exactly what they are dealing with—from waltzing into the palace (twice) and traipsing through the city wrecking things, Shuri's not sure it will come out into the open in broad daylight. Which is the only time they could attempt this considering how infrequently the princess is NOT surrounded by grown-ups.

"I really, truly, sincerely hope this works," Shuri says into the wind.

It's been three days since the intruder's last "visit" to the palace, though there have been reports of it popping up in other places throughout the kingdom. Last night, the princess spent hours creating a rough replica of the nebular gem she saw in the photo online. *That* one is a pale pink color with an iridescent sheen, and while she's not entirely sure she got the scale right, it seemed to her to be the size of an extra-large river pebble. Like a giant blush-colored marble, flattened out.

Little hunk of rose quartz, smoothed into shape by a diamond-grinding disk tool Shuri created when trying to get into making Vibranium jewelry (definitely a bust), then coated in kaleidoscopic mica powder and topped with a self-hardening glaze.

She placed a dozen teensy-tiny nanotech tracking devices across the glistening surface. If their intruder picks the thing up at all, at least one of them will stick to his hands. Then they'll be able to locate it wherever it goes.

Even K'Marah was impressed. "Wow, that is *beautiful*!" she said, holding it up to the light to take in the shimmer. "If your whole plan is a bust, will you pull the tracking thingies off and let me have it?"

Shuri had rolled her eyes then . . . her best friend just couldn't resist a shiny object.

But she's certainly not rolling them now.

"Okay, let's get started," she says to K'Marah— who is in full Dora garb today. And acting as Shuri's assistant. "I'm going to prep the drone for bait placement, and I need you to—"

"'Hold your Kimoyo card up so you can see what you're doing because you need both your hands to control the drone,'" K'Marah says. "You've only told me nine hundred and seventeen times."

"Oh hush."

Extra carefully, Shuri loads the gem into the small compartment on the underside of her drop-off drone. (She has a *pickup* one as well. It has a multi-jointed claw where this one's containment box is.) Then she powers the machine on and puts it in stealth-mode. It disappears right before the girls' eyes.

"Whoa!" K'Marah says.

"This is why we need the Kimoyo card. In stealth-mode, I can't guide the thing by sight, and I couldn't get the software to upload to my CatEyez." It had frustrated Shuri to no end, knowing she wouldn't be able to use the multipurpose glasses she invented *precisely* for tasks like this one. "Did the views from the cameras pop up?"

"Yep!" K'Marah says, holding the small screen where Shuri can see it. There are six images: one from each of the four sides of the box, giving the girls a 360-degree view, and two wide-angle ones that show what's above the shoebox-size machine and what's beneath it.

"Here goes," Shuri says, pressing the button on her controller that makes the device lift into the air. "Now hold the screen as steady as possible so I don't crash this thing."

"Aye, aye, Captain." And K'Marah puts the card in Shuri's view.

It's quite a spectacular sight, like floating over the world within a glass globe. Shuri can see the sky above and the bare earth below ... nothing grows on or around the cliffs that house the Sacred Mound. There are the mountains in the distance on one view, and the towering skyscrapers of Birnan Zana on another. She almost wants to fly the thing around Wakanda just to see what it all looks like.

"Shuri, I need to tell you something," K'Marah says, breaking the princess's reverie. The drone takes a sharp dip to the right.

"K'Marah, you can't startle me like that! We only have one chance to get this right today, and if I break our mode of faux-gem transport, there won't be a chance to try again until I build a new one."

K'Marah sighs. "Fine, fine," she replies. "But trust me when I say you'll one hundred percent want to hear this."

Shuri nods once and then refocuses on the task at hand. She chose a spot near the base of a cliff across the wide valley from where the girls are now. There is absolutely nothing significant about said spot other than the fact that it is nicely shaded and easily accessed by a narrow rift that separates it from the cliff beside it. Hopefully the symbiote is looking *everywhere* for the gem.

"Okay, we are making our initial descent," Shuri says.

This makes K'Marah giggle. The Kimoyo screen shakes.

"K'Marah!"

"Sorry, sorry. It's just that you sound like a flight attendant."

"A *what*?"

"Don't worry about it, Princess. I'm sure with all your inventions and high-tech modes of transportation, you will never encounter one. I saw it in some American movie I was watching."

"You and your American movies," Shuri replies absentmindedly. "Okay. Almost there . . ."

The drone touches down a few meters away from the face of the cliff wall, and a little cloud of dust suddenly obscures the view of the underside screen.

She exhales.

"Now to drop the package and get our drone back—"

All the camera views vanish from Shuri's Kimoyo card screen, and the beaded bracelet on her wrist begins to vibrate.

A picture of Nakia—and T'Challa's arm draped

across her shoulders, though Shuri cut the rest of *him* out of the photo—pops up as the card buzzes.

"Drat," K'Marah says. "What do we do?"

"Well, we unfortunately have to answer, don't we? Otherwise they'll get all in a tizzy and go into panic-mode. And we will probably get grounded."

"True," K'Marah says.

"Just hit the button to take the call without video—"

K'Marah taps the *wrong* button (and, fine: On Shuri's *updated* Kimoyo card, the position of the video and no-video commands are switched), and Nakia's face fills the screen. K'Marah quickly lifts it so that only she is visible. The controller in Shuri's hand would certainly raise some suspicion. "Hello, Nakia!" she says overenthusiastically.

"K'Marah, where is Shuri?"

"She's, ahhh . . ."

Shuri quicky swivels the lever that opens the drone's trapdoor and lets the fake nebular gem drop out. Then she shuts off the stealth-mode and commands the thing back into the air. Yes, someone might see it now, but she has a hunch that her access to the camera views will not be returned, and they need to get the thing back as quickly as possible.

"She's in a tree!"

Shuri's head whips left—and so does the drone. She

fumbles to course correct. Then looks at her friend again like, *What on earth are you doing?*

"She's *what*, now?" Nakia says.

K'Marah brings the card closer to her face, Shuri presumes to hide the glaringly treeless landscape behind her. "Yes. She saw some strange leaf she thought she could use for one of her experiments—you know how she is, Nakia—and despite my protests, she climbed on up!"

There's a pause. The drone is almost back to them, about the length of one of those American "football" fields left to go (such a silly name considering they mostly use their hands, in Shuri's humble opinion). Then Nakia says, "All right. Well, we need you both back here at the rear loading dock within the next ten minutes. It is time to return to the city for your mid-day meal."

Shuri shakes her head. Ever since the second break-in, Mother has insisted that she and Shuri take all major meals—breakfast, lunch, and supper—together on a palace patio. "Stall for one more minute!" she hisses at K'Marah.

"Yes! Okay, Nakia, no problem. I will let the princess know. SHURIIII! HEY, SHURI, YOU MUST GET DOWN FROM THERE AT ONCE! WE HAVE TO RETURN TO CIVILIZATION!"

"Oh boy," Shuri mouths. "Good thing her biggest dream was to become a Dora Milaje and not an actor . . ."

"See you soon, Nakia! Byyyyye!" K'Marah ends the call. "I heard what you just said, by the way," she says to Shuri. "And you're *welcome* for covering your royal butt!"

"Got it!" Shuri exclaims, landing the drone between them. She lets the tension drop from her shoulders, then moves to put the drone back in its case before shoving the whole thing into her backpack. "And thank you." She looks up at her friend and smiles. "For *all* your help."

K'Marah smiles back and lifts her chin. "Face it, Princess: You couldn't live without me."

◇◆◇◆◇

The next time Shuri's Kimoyo card starts buzzing, it's one o'clock in the morning. And since the only person who would phone her at that hour is across the room, the princess is almost certain it's not an incoming call. "Oh my gods!" she says. She puts down the textbook she's reading on her bed (nuclear physics . . . total cakewalk, but nothing wrong with a refresher) and snatches the device from the nightstand. She takes in all the flashing yellow dots on the map of Wakanda that have appeared on her screen. There are nine in the valley just outside the Sacred Mound, and a cluster of three on the move.

She looks up at K'Marah, who is flipping through some fashion magazine in the reading nook. "K'Marah!"

"Hmmm?"

Shuri taps around on the screen, and a three-dimensional holographic version of the map appears in midair.

It takes K'Marah a second to catch on, but once she does . . .

"Wait. Is that—" She gasps. Then looks right at Shuri. "It actually *worked*?"

"I mean, unless some undiscovered species of very speedy animal came in contact with our fake gem, I would say *yes*! See how fast those dots are moving? And none of the world's swiftest animals are native to our land."

"So where is it going, do you think?" K'Marah rises from her perch to circle the floating map.

"Guess we'll find out once it stops."

The girls watch as their dots zip north. They go around Birnin Bashenga to the west, then swing back east and skirt the outer edge of Wakanda's most recently developed city, Birnin T'Chaka (Shuri's heart clenches a bit at the thought of Baba).

They begin to slow, and Shuri thinks they're going to stop at the northern tip of the city, but they don't. The dots continue north.

There's only one habitable place beyond that. Well, theoretically habitable—there are people who live there, though Shuri's never *met* any of them.

Their intruder couldn't possibly be going *there* . . . could it?

"Great Bast," K'Marah says once the dot comes to rest.

"Is it living there, do you think?" Shuri asks aloud.

But K'Marah doesn't respond.

"K'Marah?" Shuri turns to her friend. The little Dora's eyes are wide, and she looks as though she has stumbled onto the Djalia and come face-to-face with the spirits of the ancestors. "K'Marah, what's the matter?"

"It went to the Jabari-Lands," K'Marah says to no one in particular.

"Yes. And what of it?"

Now K'Marah shifts her gaze to Shuri. "Remember earlier when I told you I needed to tell you something?"

Shuri's heart drops. "Yes . . . I do."

"Well, I think now is a great time for that conversation." K'Marah looks back at the map.

The dots haven't moved.

"Umm . . . okay," Shuri says. "What does it pertain to?"

K'Marah sighs then, and her shoulders drop. (Shuri hates when this happens. Always precedes some sort of bad news.)

"Shuri?" she says.

"Yes?"

K'Marah meets the princess's eyes. "I think I might know who is hosting our alien."

8

ORPHAN

By the time K'Marah stops talking, Shuri feels like a complete numskull *and* a bad friend.

For one, the little Dora lets the princess know that she'd *tried* to relay the whole story while they were in the Necropolis safe house. But halfway through, she realized her sole audience member was asleep. ("You are insufferable, Shuri," she says before starting from the top.)

"About a week ago, I received a cryptic message from a number I didn't recognize. *'Think something may be wrong,'* is what it said. So I did what I always do when this happens: I sent a reply that simply read, *'New phone. Who dis?'* Your good friend Riri Williams actually taught me the tactic. It's apparently all the rage on that side of the pond."

Shuri smacks her forehead but doesn't say a word.

"Anyhow, then I get *another* message, and *this* one read . . . actually, hold that thought." She goes over to the reading nook to grab her Kimoyo card, then comes back to join Shuri on the bed. "You can just read it." She taps the screen so that the message thread appears in the air the same way the map did.

Shuri scans through:

Tue 19 Feb 20:32

Unknown

I am sure you would prefer

not to hear from me.

But think something may be wrong.

New phone. Who dis?

This is Henny.

But PLEASE don't be alarmed!

. . .

WOW do YOU have nerve!

Didn't I tell you to LOSE my number?

Last I checked, you poisoned me?

I know, I know. And I am so sorry.

I truly didn't want to . . .

> As if that actually matters?

> I should've gone with my gut . . .

> BLOCK!

K'Marah, please please please don't.

> Why shouldn't I, Henny? Hmm?

> Give me ONE good reason.

I don't have a good reason.

I just . . . I really need your help.

I went to great lengths to acquire this device.

I could be exiled from this community for

even using it.

This is THAT important. Please.

> You have three minutes, Henbane.

> Then I am going back to pretending

> that you do not exist and that I know

> nothing at all about you.

> Go.

Thank you, thank you.

This is going to sound strange . . .

But for the past three days, I have woken

up extremely tired.

Almost as though . . . I ran a great distance

in my sleep.

My muscles ache and I wake with a terrible

headache.

Sounds like a personal problem to me.

Well, yes.

But I also have these . . . dreams.

1.5 minutes left.

Which is why I am contacting you.

Last night, I dreamed that I was running

through the royal palace.

Where your friend lives.

My friend's NAME is Shuri.

And she is the PRINCESS of this nation.

I meant no disrespect . . .

Anyway, when I woke up this morning

my legs were so sore, I struggled to move

them.

Your time is up, Henbane.

K'Marah, wait!

Please!

K'Marah?

"Wow. You left him on *read*? Harsh."

"Did you *read* the thread, Shuri? He said he dreamed he was running through the palace!" K'Marah exclaims. "And he woke up with sore legs!"

Now Shuri begins to pick up what K'Marah is laying down. "Hold on. Are you suggesting . . . ? No way, K'Marah."

"I received these messages the day after the initial break-in, Shuri!" K'Marah goes on. "I will admit that the first time I tried to relay this, at some point during the telling, I closed my eyes and must've drifted off to sleep as well. When I woke, the creature—Henbane bonded with the weirdo symbiote, I'm guessing—was standing there, staring at us. And you didn't say a word about what I'd told you—"

"Because I didn't hear it."

"Yes, I know that *now*, but before, I thought it was because you didn't think it was worth any further conversation."

The princess's eyes narrow as she tries to absorb what her friend is saying. "So you think Henbane is the host?" she asked. "Based solely on these messages?"

"Well, that's the thing." The text thread vanishes from the air. "When you didn't make a fuss about it the first time, I decided to let the whole thing go. Blocked him like I should've done ages ago." She throws her hands into the air. (*So* dramatic.)

"Okay . . ."

"Well, then *last* night, he sent me a direct message on one of my social media accounts."

"Oh my word, K'Marah. You make yourself so unnecessarily vulnerable."

"Only *he* knows that I am actually *me* there. Anyway, that message sounded even more dire. He basically begged me for help. Said he felt like he might be losing his mind, and he has no one else to turn to. That he'd dreamed about being inside the palace again."

"All right . . ."

"And *then* he said something that I didn't think made any sense: '*If she has it, tell her to just give it to him.*'"

Now Shuri's eyes go wide. "Wait, really?"

"It didn't occur to me that what I was hearing from him and what we're doing with this whole alien intruder thing could be connected until I saw the fake gem just before you put it inside the drone," she says. "And then I tried to just shake it off. But some of the things Mr. Fury told us about how the creature works—binding itself to a host, and even being able to use that host without its awareness . . . Remember what he said about the Venom one using Spider-Man's body at nighttime to do its *own* bidding—"

"And Spider-Man waking up the next day, completely exhausted . . ." Shuri says, finishing K'Marah's thought. She thinks for a moment and then shakes her head. "I don't know, K'Marah. I hear everything you're saying, but . . ."

"Come *on*, Shuri. *Think* about it. There are too many pieces that fit!" K'Marah reaches over and taps Shuri's card so that the map pops into the air again. The three dots haven't budged from their spot in the mountains where the Jabari reside. "We know Henbane returned to the Jabari-Lands once he was pardoned—"

"I still can't believe my brother just let him off the hook like that," Shuri gripes. "Anyway, continue."

"Whatever your tracking devices got attached to is currently in the Jabari-Lands. Just . . . *chilling*."

"Figuratively *and* literally," Shuri chimes in. The mountain range where the Jabari make their home is *always* snowcapped.

"Yes," K'Marah replies. "That was the point of the pun." She shakes her head. "As I was saying, what Henbane describes in his messages aligns with what Mr. Fury told us about the aliens."

"Okay, fine," Shuri replies. "But Fury also told us the symbiote chooses its specific host for a reason. Why, exactly, would one choose a boy who isn't even *Wakandan* to go ripping through *Wakanda* in search of some mystical gem?"

"I mean, you said the last person known to have it was that Zanda lady, no? And she's Narobian. Makes perfect sense to me that a symbiote could bind with a kid who seemed to spend a lot of time with her. Especially if there is truth in what Fury said about symbiote thingies having access to their host's memories."

Shuri opens her mouth to respond with a rebuttal . . . but then closes it. Because she doesn't have one. Based on the various snippets of evidence, K'Marah's theory *does* make a significant amount of sense.

"How do we find out for sure?" she asks her friend, turning to her.

"Well, *that* part I don't really know. I doubt texting *'Hey, that whole give-it-to-him thing you mentioned . . . were you saying that because you're being possessed by an alien in your sleep?'* would yield a simple yes or no."

"Valid," Shuri replies. And then she yawns. "Guess we can sleep on it."

"Yeah," K'Marah says absentmindedly.

And though the princess can tell K'Marah has more on her mind, she decides not to pry this time. "Good night," she says, climbing into bed.

"Mm-hmm," comes the reply from her little Dora.

◇◇◇◇

Shuri's Kimoyo card is blaring.

"I swear that thing won't let me *live*," K'Marah says groggily from beside Shuri. "Yesterday, it interrupted our Very Important Mission. Today it's interrupting our sleep."

Shuri groans and forces her eyes open to check the time: 10:27 a.m.

The ringing stops—

And then starts right back up again. Which is when Shuri really *hears* it . . . and sits bolt upright. Because that specific ring sound is set to just one number: Mother's.

And she rarely calls.

"Shuriiiii," K'Marah complains. "Must you *move* so much?" She pulls a pillow over her head.

Ignoring her friend, the princess takes a centering breath and then answers on speakerphone. "Ahh . . . Shuri's phone! How may I help—"

"Shuri, please come to the throne room at once."

And then she—the poised, etiquette-driven queen of Wakanda—hangs up without waiting for a response.

"Dang," K'Marah says, now sitting up as well. "Guess that's *my* cue to leave."

"Noooo! Don't leave me, K'Marah!"

"Sorry, Princess," the young Dora replies as she rolls out of bed to gather her things. "She sounded peeved. You're on your own this time."

There's a knock at Shuri's door.

"Uhhh . . . come in!" she shouts, trying (and failing) to keep the quaver out of her voice.

Nakia pokes her head in. "Your immediate presence is requested in the throne room, Your Majesty."

K'Marah pulls on her boots and makes a beeline for the door. "Byyyyyyye!" she trills like a gloating songbird. "Call me later, okay? *If* you survive, that is . . ."

"K'Marah!" Shuri shouts behind her. "Not helpful!"

Nakia laughs. "Come on, Shuri. Let's go before your mother calls again."

Shuri sighs.

As she makes her way through the halls in her pajamas (again)—with Nakia in front of her, and a Dora Shuri's never met bringing up the rear—Shuri runs through all the things she could potentially be in trouble for this time. Had someone seen her drone yesterday morning? Had Mother somehow come to discover that her daughter had a full-blown *conversation* with the havoc-wreaking being who is currently Wakanda's Most Wanted, and then hadn't told her? Had Fury called Ramonda and told her everything he'd been discussing with her daughter?

As the doors loom larger, so does what feels like a plutonium sphere inside Shuri's belly. It's the heaviest known metal in the universe, and with each step, Shuri feels like bits of it are seeping into her shoes, making it increasingly difficult for her to move her legs.

Just before the doors swing open, Shuri takes a deep breath that *feels* like it might be one of her last. She drops her eyes to the floor as she crosses the threshold into the cavernous space. Mother will certainly take issue with her entering the throne room without her back straight and chin aloft, but Shuri is sure *this* infraction pales in comparison with whatever transgression she was brought in for.

Nakia stops and moves to Shuri's right side, while the new Dora flanks the princess on the left. She can see the queen's ornately beaded, pointy-toed shoes.

"Shuri—"

"Whatever it is, Mother, I can assure you that it won't happen again," Shuri blurts, lifting her head to meet Mother's eyes.

They look rather puzzled. "What on earth are you talking about, child?" she asks.

Which is when she notices that Mother is not alone.

There's a boy beside her—not *too*, too tall but certainly tall enough. Brown skin, black hair that's a bit curly on the top, but faded on the sides. Jeans, gray T-shirt with *Brooklyn Visions Academy* scrawled across it in white beneath a black-and-red hooded jacket. If

Shuri had to guess, she'd say he was about fifteen.

And he's holding a wrapped box.

"As I was saying before you interrupted me . . ." She flashes the princess a humorless smile that lets her know there will be a *discussion* about this at a more opportune time. "You, my dear, have a visitor."

MISSION LOG

I . . . HAVE A VISITOR.

His name is Miles Morales, and I was correct in my estimation of his age: fifteen. He traveled all the way here from his home in Brooklyn, New York.

And he came bearing gifts! I must admit: The way he bowed and said, "I present a most humble gift to you, Princess Shuri of Wakanda. I hope it is to your liking," as he shoved the beautifully wrapped and ribboned box in my direction, was rather cute. In fact, HE is rather cute . . . But I digress.

Within the box was a lovely beaded necklace and earring set, a bag of assorted candies Miles referred to as "dulces"

("The guava ones are MY personal favorite," he said), and a second box marked by the silhouette of a man who appeared to be mid-jumping split with one hand straight up in the air. THAT box contained a pair of shoes unlike any I have ever seen before. They are red, black, and white with an oddly curved check mark on the side, and they lace up on top of the foot and come up over the ankle.

"They're 1s," he said.

"Wons?"

"Yeah, 1s. Jordan 1s."

"Jordan won what?" (Bast, how utterly embarrassing!)

"The shoes are Air Jordan 1s. Like the *number* one." He pointed at his own feet then. "See? They match mine."

As it turns out, this Miles Morales was SENT here by one Nicholas Joseph Fury with the blessing of my Super-Hero-mission-preferring brother.

And no clue exactly what Fury told T'Challa about Miles to gain his clearance—or what T'Challa told Mother—but whatever it was, Mother welcomed Miles with open arms and put him in the most lavish of all the palace guest suites.

The MOST bizarre thing: Once I'd opened my gifts, Mother told Ayo to walk us to the palace library. "Good luck with your task, Miles," she said. "We are thrilled that you have come to assist us, and I have no doubt my beloved daughter will be most helpful." And she WINKED at me.

I don't know that I have ever been so befuddled . . .

That is, until we reached the library, and Ayo left us alone.

The minute she was gone, I rounded on him. "All right, who are you, and what in Bast's name is going on?" (Not my proudest moment, but all the peculiarity was beginning to grate.)

"Wait, Fury didn't tell you?" he asked.

"Tell me *what*, precisely?"

"That I was coming."

"Ahh . . . no."

"Unbelievable," he said, shaking his head.

Within fifteen or so minutes, I'd heard a series of facts that were so outlandish, had I not been in the thick of some of them with full knowledge of their truth, I might've called for Ayo and asked her to have him escorted by armed guard back to whatever mode of transport T'Challa utilized to get him here. But if even part of what he said was true, I knew it all had to be.

Including the part about why Fury sent *him*: This Miles is somewhat of an expert when it comes to Klyntar symbiotes.

While he was a bit mum with regard to details, Miles told me that he had experience interacting with the symbiote before and was intimately familiar with how the Klyntar function and what their weaknesses are.

But then he said: "Now, I gotta be up front with you: I've had, ummm . . . very *different* encounters with it. One not TOO bad, but the other . . ." His eyes narrowed then. "Well, that one I won't even talk about. Point being, from what I'VE experienced, the symbiotes are about as predictable as Kyrie Irving with a rock in his hand."

I had no idea what he was talking about.

Me: "Ahhh . . . So how exactly can YOU help?"

Miles: "Dang. Way to hit a guy right in the self-esteem."

Me: "No, I didn't mean—"

Miles: "It's fine, it's fine. If nothing else, I can help you figure this one out so we can decide what to do about it."

Me: "Okaaaay . . ."

Miles: "Have a little faith in me, yeah? Fury sure seems to. He's got faith in you, too."

Which brought me to the question that was *really* burning me alive. "By the way: What exactly *did* Fury tell my brother?"

Miles shrugged. "No idea. Had to be similar to what he told my mom. *Something* made her agree to let me fly halfway around the world to a country nobody's even heard of."

"Wait, so your parents don't know why you are really here?"

"Nope. There's, uhh . . . a lot some of the people closest to me are in the proverbial dark about."

(Feels ridiculous now, but in the moment, I was impressed with his word choice.)

"Huh."

"He said—and I quote—'I *am completely confident that you, the princess, and her feisty young friend can handle this matter. Involve the queen only if you absolutely* have *to.*'"

"*Really?*" I replied. "Mr. *Fury* said that?"

"Verbatim."

"Wow."

"That being said, we should probably get started," he went on. "My mom is expecting me to come home in seven days."

"Seven *days?!* What on earth are we supposed to accomplish in seven days?"

"Well," he said. "The hope is that we're gonna get rid of an alien."

9
GAME PLAN

K'Marah is initially no help at all. The moment Shuri
introduces Miles, the Dora Karami's eyes glaze
over and her head drops to one side as she sighs.

The entire first hour the trio spend in the library—
which, as it turns out, is the only space in the entire
nation that Mother will permit Shuri to be without a
guard (or two) glued to her side—all K'Marah does
is stare. Shuri is the person who relays K'Marah's
Henbane-as-host theory, and it's not until Miles asks
the little Dora something specific that she pulls her
act together.

"Okay, so . . . this Henbane guy," he begins. "You were dating him?"

"I mean, I wouldn't call it *dating* per se," she replies (vaguely flustered, which makes Shuri hide a chuckle behind her hand). "But, yes, we were well acquainted. Or at least I *thought* we were . . ." Her face clouds over with fury then.

"Got it. So . . . what can you tell me about him? Like, based on what you believed to be true?"

"Well, there are certainly some things Shuri and I *know* to be true based on our initial encounter with him. Like, he's Narobian by birth—"

"Narobian?" Miles asks, eyes narrowing. (Okay. He *is* cute.)

Shuri cuts in. "Narobia is a small nation approximately three hundred kilometers—or about two hundred miles based on the bizarre measurements you use in your country—due west, on the other side of Canaan. It is ruled by a highly delusional woman—"

"*Evil giantess* is more accurate, but carry on," K'Marah says. It makes Miles laugh.

"Yes, well . . . she has quite the vendetta against *our* nation and recently sought to invade and over-take it."

"Sheesh," from Miles.

"So Henbane—and of course I didn't know *any* of this when he and I initially connected online—was actually being *used* by this wicked and unnecessarily large nation-invader, Princess Zanda," K'Marah says. "He is a—what is the proper term, Shuri?"

"A mutant."

"Ah, okay!" Miles says. "There's this lady Fury introduced me to recently, Wanda Maximoff. It's *wild* seeing what she can do with a little wiggle of her fingers. What's your ex's special ability?"

"He is *not* my ex," K'Marah snaps, leaning forward as if to strike, cobra-style.

"Whoa, whoa!" Miles lifts his hands in surrender. "My bad! Don't karate chop me or anything!"

Shuri laughs. "He has this interesting power over organic matter. Can kill just about any plant with a single touch, and can also use the toxin his body produces and releases through his hands to knock a person unconscious."

"Dang," Miles says.

"He's also an orphan," K'Marah adds. "No known family in Narobia, though he *was* taken in by our nation's Jabari."

"The Jabari are a tribe of Wakandans who make their home in the high mountains," Shuri explains before Miles can ask. "They keep themselves cut off from the rest of Wakandan society and shun the use of technology."

"Something Henbane clearly did *not* adhere to." K'Marah looks away and crosses her arms.

"Okay, so he's an orphan from another country who lives in a place with people who have cut themselves off from your society. Did I get all that right?"

"You did," Shuri says. "And K'Marah has theorized that the alien being chose him as a host because of his affiliation with Princess—"

"Evil giantess."

"Excuse me: evil giantess Zanda." Shuri looks at K'Marah as if to say, *Happy now?* "Zanda, apparently, is the last person to possess the object our symbiote is after."

"But it—he—didn't go to her first?" Miles asks, very clearly just as puzzled about this as Shuri was/*is*. "Why does he even want this gem thing?"

The princess shrugs. "No idea. All we know for sure is that he's *here*, scouring the country in search of it. My *vaguely* educated guess is that he—the symbiote, that is—wants to go somewhere. Based on the limited information I acquired, this nebular gem gives the bearer an ability to teleport through means that aren't *quite* scientifically sound. Not that extraterrestrial objects have to adhere to *our* limited understanding of physics."

"This much is true." Miles nods. It makes Shuri's heart swell. "So do we know where he is now?" Miles continues.

Shuri lifts her wrist and taps a bead on her bracelet. A full Wakandan landscape leaps into the air.

"Whoa!" Miles says. "How did . . . ?"

"The technology is quite simple," Shuri remarks. "I'll explain later. You see those two groupings of dots?" She points out the nine that have been transported to a spot in the forest (definitely an animal's doing) and the three that are currently moving from the base of the mountains in the direction of Birnan T'Chaka. "We're pretty sure *that's* him."

"Looks about right," Miles says. "Though I'm not sure how I feel about the fact that this one moves as fast as Venom."

"Did you presume he'd be slower?" Shuri asks.

"Wishful thinking, I suppose." Miles's eyes narrow. "And I'm guessing that since you know the potential host, you don't wanna, like . . . take him out of the game completely, right?"

"Game?" Shuri replies. "What game?"

"Oh my gods, Princess," comes K'Marah's exasperated voice. "He means take him out as in eliminate his existence. As in kill him—"

"Bast, no!" Shuri exclaims. "We merely want to capture the being and get him *out* of Wakanda."

"Okay. Well, I know a little bit about how to make the symbiote separate from the host, and what kind of apparatus would be needed to contain it. But umm . . . well, full disclosure here: I've never tried to *catch* a symbiote. So not entirely sure how to pull *that* part off."

"Duly noted," Shuri says. "We can figure that out together. However, before we talk about *how* to catch him, we need to figure out *where*."

◈◈◈◈◈

If Shuri thought Miles was blown away by her hovering 3-D topographical map, she had no idea: When the Brooklyn-born, brown-skinned boy lays eyes on the hoverjet that will fly them around Wakanda for his aerial tour, he gets so excited, his voice cracks. "Oh my god, bro. This is *so* awesome!"

"Too bad we can't take him around in the *Predator*," K'Marah whispers to Shuri.

"It truly is tragic," Shuri replies. Not that they hadn't *asked* to take him around in Shuri's personal, Panther-shaped transport vessel (with a cloaking mechanism that makes it all but invisible, no less). Mother had given Shuri that tight-lipped smile she reserves for times when she'd like to throttle her. "Don't press your luck," she said. "Hoverjet with Ayo, or stay home."

So here they are. All three squeezed into the passenger cabin, with K'Marah seated in the middle. That way Miles can see out the window and Shuri can explain what he's seeing from the view *she* has.

"Wow. It's really beautiful here," Miles says. "So much . . . *green*."

Shuri swells with pride. "Is the land barren where you are from?"

"Land?" Miles snorts. "What land? Not much where I'm from but buildings."

"Ah."

"Is that other place like this?" Miles continues. "Narobia, I think you said it's called?"

"I—"

"It isn't," K'Marah cuts in. "I've never been on the ground there, but I did fly over it a number of times during my Dora Milaje training. Narobia *is* rather barren. That's partially why Zanda attacked us. She felt that we were too . . . *stingy*, I think you say in your country, with our resources."

"Hmm," Miles replies. But doesn't expound.

Shuri isn't sure what to say to that.

Turns out she doesn't have to say anything at all.

"Reason I ask that . . . I've been thinkin' a little

more about why a symbiote would've chosen your boy to bond with."

"He's NOT my *boy*—"

"I know, I know. That's just an expression we use back home."

"What conclusion did you come to?" Shuri asks, trying to get the conversation back on the rails. She looks out the window. "Oh, by the way: We are currently flying over Birnan Djata," she says, pointing to the small city beneath them. It's slightly less shiny and spectacle-like than the capital, but certainly no less impressive. The architect responsible for the tallest and most extravagant buildings in the capital had her way here, too.

"That's dope," Miles says. "Where is the target right now?"

Shuri checks her Kimoyo card. Not quite enough space in their part of the jet to launch the full landscape hologram. "Still in the mountains. According to what our potential host told K'Marah, it would seem the symbiote gets on the move mostly after the sun goes down."

"And from the way it sounded," K'Marah cuts in, "Henbane isn't necessarily *conscious* when his body is . . . being 'used,' for lack of a better term."

"Interesting," Miles replies. "Well, like I said, I was thinking about some of the stuff Fury told me in light of *my* encounters with Venom. This is gonna sound weird, but he apparently chooses hosts he has something in common with, like . . . emotionally."

"Huh?" Shuri asks.

"So the guy he was bonded with after Spider-Man, Eddie Brock? Venom allegedly chose *him* because they had a shared hatred of Spider-Man. Like Spider-Man—who *brought* Venom here in the first place, mind you—rejected Venom at one point, and that supposedly damaged Venom's self-esteem."

"Ummm . . ."

"Right. Definitely weird that the thing even *has* self-esteem. Anyway, it was attracted to Eddie because Eddie also hated Spider-Man. Spider-Man ruined Eddie's life when he revealed that something Eddie reported on was Fake News."

"Is that a thing?" K'Marah asks.

"Sadly is in America. Whole thing torched Eddie's journalism career."

"Dang," from K'Marah.

"Crossing over Birnan T'Chaka now," Shuri says. "It's relatively new. And is named for my baba. It is the closest in appearance to the capital city."

"It's, like . . . kinda sparkly," Miles says.

Shuri laughs. "Yeah. I guess it is. Go on with what you were saying?"

"Yeah, okay. My theory is that even beyond the whole thing with the Narobian kid having had contact with the lady who last had this *gem* the symbiote is looking for, I wonder if he also picked the kid because of, like . . . shared loneliness. And feeling like a stranger in a strange land?" Miles says. "Not that this land is particularly *strange* . . . Just—you get what I'm saying? Alien on earth, Narobian orphan in Wakanda . . ."

Shuri digests the suggestion. "That's a pretty solid theory," she says. "Now just to figure out how to use it to our advantage. If it turns out to be true, of course."

"Right."

"We have almost reached the Jabari-Lands," Ayo's voice says over the intercom. "We will not fly over out of respect for their customs and privacy, but you can see the snow-covered mountains quite clearly through your respective windows—"

"Oh no," Shuri says.

"What?" from K'Marah. Who looks far more alarmed than necessary. "What happened?"

"Well, nothing happened, per se. It's just occurring to me that this mission might be more difficult than we presumed."

"How so?" the Dora asks. "Can't we just go in during the daytime when the symbiote appears to be inactive and, like . . . capture it?"

"That *sounds* simple enough . . . but we can't *fly* over because of their customs—which reject all forms of technology and modern conveniences. I would venture to guess that *all* forms of modern transport would be forbidden to use in this region."

"Which would mean . . . ?" Miles says.

"We'll have to enter Jabari-Lands on foot. And, like . . . hike."

"But you're the *princess*, Shuri," K'Marah says. "First in line to the throne. Don't all these people in this land have to do whatever you say?"

Shuri shakes her head. "We are not that kind of royal family, K'Marah. We honor and respect *all* Wakandans and their individual customs."

Miles looks impressed. "That's pretty dope," he says. "Wish it was like that where I come from."

"Okay. Fine," from K'Marah. "Your benevolence is duly noted. Hiking will take longer, obviously, but anything is possible with the right pair of shoes."

"You are forgetting one very important factor, Dora Karami," Shuri replies.

"And what's that?" from Miles.

"My mother," Shuri says. "There is no way *I* would be permitted to go anywhere *near* the Jabari-Lands without at least one guard. And especially not for an extended period of time. Do see exhibit A." She gestures to the soundproof window where Ayo appears to be chatting happily with the pilot on the other side of it.

"Oh, this is easy," K'Marah says with a dismissive wave of her hand. Her collection of gold bangles clink against one another and make a chime-like sound that is not entirely ridiculous.

Though what the little Dora just said certainly is. "What do you mean, *easy*?" Shuri says. "You have *met* my mother, yes?"

"No, *really*. This won't be as complicated as you're anticipating."

"Oh, *please* do tell."

The Dora Karami pats her friend's knee then. "There are loopholes, Your Majesty."

"Okay . . . and they are?"

"We can get into the details later," she says. "My point is that we need a grown-up, and I know precisely how to get us one. Who won't tattle."

"Sounds good to me," Miles says.

Shuri has no idea how to respond to that.

"Yep!" from K'Marah. "Now, let's all kick back and enjoy the remainder of this flight."

10

GROWN-UP

Shuri does her best to temper her frustrations over the fact that, yet again, her Dora Karami best friend knows more about the inner workings of royal protocols than she does. Because, as it turns out, K'Marah is right: Getting a grown-up really *will* be much easier than the princess would've imagined.

Post tour and a short supper, Miles immediately retired to his suite. ("Man, that whole jet lag thing is no joke," he said with a yawn.) So the girls are alone in Shuri's quarters and free to discuss whatever they please.

"So one of the rules," K'Marah says while stretched

out on her back, staring up at the elaborate canopy above Shuri's bed, "is that any Dora Milaje who is granted the Msingi title in relation to a specific royal takes an oath to attend and protect that royal above all others."

"Okay . . ."

"That protection includes said royal's secrets." K'Marah sits up on her elbows and looks at the princess. Who is sitting in the book nook, pretending to read a book on diplomatic conflict resolution. (Fitting.)

"According to the oath, a Msingi is sworn to secrecy about *anything* their royal doesn't want others to know—your mother and brother included."

Shuri doesn't know whether to be excited to learn this, or furious about not knowing it. "So . . . why don't I have one of those?"

"You haven't asked." K'Marah shrugs. "The designation and assignment are given to a Dora only if they are requested by a particular royal."

Now Shuri *is* mad. "Why didn't you tell me this *before*, K'Marah? All the sneaking around we've done, and we could've just taken an adult with us the whole time??"

"I didn't learn it until I was promoted to Dora Karami!" she says. "And frankly, even after I *did* learn it, I'm not sure it would've ever occurred to me to tell you. You're . . . not the biggest fan of grown-ups? Especially when you are trying to accomplish something. You have complained many times about them 'just getting in the way and slowing everything down.'"

And Shuri doesn't respond. Because K'Marah is absolutely right.

They do wind up losing an entire day: Shuri goes to Mother to put in her request before bed. And of course Mother is wildly suspicious, but she does Kimoyo-call T'Challa . . . whose hologram groggily waves off her concern. "Okoye became my Msingi when I was twelve years old, Mother. Shuri will be perfectly all right," he says with a yawn. (*What time zone is he in?*) "I am certain you trust our incredible warrior women to do what they are trained for and keep Shuri safe, no?"

Mother relents, but solely under the condition that *she* will choose Shuri's assigned companion. Which of course makes the princess very nervous—what if Mother chooses someone endlessly strict and intimidating? Or worse: overcautious?

However, what can the princess do but agree?

"You will know of my selection by this time tomorrow evening," Mother says on Shuri's way out of the queen's quarters. It takes everything in the princess not to balk or openly panic about the time crunch (and she could swear she hears Mother mutter, *"Who on earth even told her about the Msingi designation?"* as she leaves).

As it turns out, though, the "lost" day winds up being quite beneficial. Because there is something Shuri failed to consider until Miles mentions it in the library after breakfast the following morning: "Okay, so what are we catching him with?"

"Huh?" Shuri and K'Marah say in tandem.

"The symbiote. We need something to contain it, or this whole mission is pointless."

"Hmm," K'Marah says, much more focused today. "Definitely wouldn't have thought of that."

"That's what I'm here for." And he winks. (Now the little Dora looks like she might faint out of her chair.) "So what are our options?"

"Ahhh . . . what do the specifications need to be?" Shuri says. And though she's nervous at first—the mention of containment merely spawns a series of new questions about the *nature* of the symbiote itself—the more Miles talks, the better she feels.

Over the next ten minutes, he explains:

1. How the symbiote functions: "Without a host, it's just like . . . an amorphous blob the color of tar. But

one that can think and feel. *With* a host, it appears as like a full-coverage suit. Similar to the one I . . . I mean Spider-Man, wears, actually. Which is mad creepy if you think about it: an alien that can envelop your whole body and look like clothes?" He shudders.

2. Its most interesting ability: "It has these really wild empathetic abilities. Where it can both read the needs, desires, and emotions of the host, and also project its own needs, desires, and emotions. I think this is partially why it seeks out a host it can already identify with. Also: The longer a host is exposed to a symbiote, the more the host's feelings and desires fall in line with the symbiote's. Gets hairy if the symbiote is a bad guy. Trust me on this one." And his eyes cloud over, though the princess doesn't dare to ask why.

3. What its weaknesses are: "Loud noise and high heat. Like fire-temperature high."

4. How to contain it: "We'd need something truly impenetrable. Like no solid, liquid, or gas could get into or out of it, and it would need to seal up reeaaaal tight."

And that's all Shuri needs to hear. "Got it."

◆◆◆◆

"*Voilà!*"

A hoverjet trip to her lab and some hours later, Shuri emerges from lab station three to find her best friend and American visitor eating snacks and playing . . . Uno.

"Hey, hey, she lives!" Miles says without looking up. "Also: BOOM. Draw four! Color is red . . . *and* UNO!"

"You are totally cheating," K'Marah grumbles as she picks up her cards.

"Don't hate the playa, small warrior. Hate the game. Uno and OUT." He smacks his red three down onto the jumbled pile of cards with far more force than seems necessary to the princess.

"Ahhh . . . Not to disturb your *leisure*, but LOOK!" Shuri sticks out the transparent cube she's been working on for . . . "Wait. What is the hour now?"

"It's"—Miles looks at his watch—"ten forty-three

a.m. back home, which would make it . . . six forty-three p.m. here."

"Six forty-three?!" Shuri exclaims. She was in the lab station for seven solid hours?? "Oh my gods, I am going to be *so* grounded. Mother *hates* when I miss supper—"

"Supper was delivered an hour ago," K'Marah says. "When the on-duty Dora knocked to tell us it was time to go eat, Miles pointed out that you were still working. So your mother had food sent straight from the palace kitchen."

"It was real good, too," Miles says. "Luwombo is what it's called, right?"

"Mm-hmm," K'Marah replies. "With gonja. Which is Shuri's favorite."

"We call it fried plantains back home," Miles says. "Well . . . in English. Whenever my mom fries them, she calls them *maduros*. And makes them with garlic."

"Your plate is in the kitchen," K'Marah says to Shuri, then "Rematch?" to Miles.

But Miles is staring at what Shuri's holding (and *trying* to show them). "That's . . . what *is* that?"

"OH! Yes!" She lifts it into the air. It's about the size of two shoeboxes stacked on top of each other. "Behold! I call it the host hexahedron!"

K'Marah smacks her forehead. "Great Bast, you are *terrible* at naming things, Shuri."

"Oh, whatever."

Miles cocks his head to one side. "I can see straight through it . . . but there's, like, a . . . shimmery-ness?"

Shuri smiles. "That's the Vibranium!"

"Whoa," Miles replies. "No clue what that means, but it sounds amazing."

The princess and K'Marah both laugh. "I decided to go with polycarbonate for the structure," Shuri continues, "and then I coated each panel on both sides with a layer of ultra-thin Vibranium contact paper I invented. Vibranium *absorbs* sound, so when you mentioned the symbiote's sonic sensitivity, I thought to myself: What better way to get it to enter the box of its own accord than by bombarding the specimen with high-frequency noise, and providing a nice little sound-proof box it can 'escape' into? Once it's inside, we let the hidden-hinged lid"—she lifts it so they can see—"snap closed, sealing the cube shut. And there you have it: contained. In a non-porous, practically indestructible receptacle."

Miles's gaze shifts from the box to Shuri's face. "You're like *maaaad* smart," he says.

It makes her face warm. "Thanks."

"Okay, this is all well and good, and she *is* highly

intelligent," K'Marah cuts in. "But once it's in there, what do we *do* with it?"

The princess ponders for a moment. It's not that she hasn't considered this. She just . . . hasn't the vaguest idea. It's why she built the cube to *last*. "That part, I'm not entirely sure," she replies, "but we can cross that bridge when we get to it. Who's ready to catch an alien?"

◇◇◇◇◇

Despite being proud of the symbiote containment cube she created, Shuri's confidence and excitement both wane as the hovercar transporting the trio gets closer to the palace. They still don't have the clearance to *go* anywhere. Nor a plan for how to *use* it. And there are only four days left to get this accomplished before Miles has to return to his Brooklyn.

Also plaguing her is K'Marah's question about what to do with the symbiote if they do manage to catch it—K'Marah who has gone home and left Shuri alone with her spiraling thoughts and no one to process through them with. Miles fell asleep en route to the palace and had to be practically carried to his room.

So she paces the length of her quarters, kneading and stretching a chunk of Vibranium-enhanced putty.

What *will* they do with it? Is she supposed to just . . . keep it here? Is she supposed to send it back to

America with Miles? Would it be possible for her to *study* it?

She remembers the way the symbiote—who's been lying low over the past couple of days—spoke to her and K'Marah. How it seemed to experience complex emotions and clearly possessed the capacity to get offended. Miles mentioned that the creatures have empathetic abilities . . . but would it be able to *feel* *without* a host?

The more Shuri thinks about it, the more she wonders if Miles is correct about their symbiote choosing Henbane because of some shared sense of unbelonging. Of having no real *home*. Does the alien being want the gem so he can disintegrate himself back to his planet of origin? Or does he have something else in mind?

There's a knock on the door.

"Come in," Shuri says absentmindedly.

She continues to pace. Kneading. Stretching. Pulling.

A throat clears, and she looks up. There's a grin on the face of the Dora who just entered the room.

"Oh, sorry. Am I being summoned?" Shuri says.

"You are not," the woman replies, cool as a cucumber.

"Is there . . . something you need?"

"Nothing in particular. Just here to do my job."

Of course Mother would request that a Dora post *inside* Shuri's quarters after the princess missed supper. Of course.

"So when and where do we begin?" the Dora asks.

"Huh? What do you mean?"

"I presume we are going on some grand adventure, yes?"

Shuri panics. "A . . . grand adventure?"

"Yes. One I imagine will involve a significant measure of danger and time away from the palace?"

Shuri doesn't know how to respond to that.

"That was the reason your brother requested a Msingi when he and I were around your age."

At the sound of that magic word, Shuri's ears perk up. And seeing who's in front of her reignites her excitement. Cautiously.

"Is this your way of telling me that *you* are going to be my Msingi, Nakia?"

Shuri's favorite Dora bows. "At your service, Your Majesty," she says. "Now, when do we depart?"

11

BASHENGA

Of course the queen mother *insists* on an extravagant royal breakfast the following morning before anyone is permitted to embark on any adventures.

"I . . . don't think I've ever been inside this room before," K'Marah whispers to Shuri as they enter the grand dining hall. It's the one used when Mother and T'Challa have *extra*-special visitors. "It is . . . WOW!"

And though Shuri huffs her annoyance, there is no denying that the Dora Karami—who is in full uniform today—is absolutely right in her one-word assessment.

The space is breathtaking. It's smaller than one would expect—"Makes for an intimate dining experience and encourages authentic conversation," T'Challa told Shuri the first time *she* came in here. She'd commented on how small it seemed compared with the main dining hall: a space with multiple long tables that seat one hundred guests each.

In here, though, there's a dome-shaped ceiling covered in hand-painted scenes of pivotal moments in Wakandan history: from the crash of the Vibranium meteorite; to the war between the tribes; to Bast leading a single warrior to the heart-shaped herb; to the uniting of the tribes beneath the single ruler and Black Panther Bashenga; to the nation moving into a period of growth and development that hasn't abated.

There are a pair of chandeliers made from a special type of crystal found only in a series of caves near the Sacred Mound. ("They're so *sparkly*," K'Marah says, gaping.)

There are gold sconces on the wall emitting appropriately golden light, beautifully patterned handwoven fabrics swooped and draped on the walls, and, at the center of the space, a round moabi-wood table surrounded by six colorfully patterned, ultra-plush armchairs.

The party of five—Shuri, her two friends, her

Msingi, and the queen mother—take their seats, and the six-course meal (*total* overkill) commences with Mother attempting to weasel information out of all of them for the duration.

She asks Miles if he's enjoying his stay, and then: "Which parts of the country will you be seeing today?"

He truthfully tells her he has no idea.

So she shifts to K'Marah: "You look so *elegant* in your official garments, Dora Karami. What adventures will you be getting into with your new designation, hmm?"

K'Marah nails the response: "Oh, *adventuring* is no longer my priority, Your Majesty. I intend solely to serve and protect your family and this nation as my oath requires." With a reverent nod of her head. (Ha!)

Undeterred, the queen mother moves on to Nakia: "Should be a rousing good time with these youngsters, eh?" She winks. "Are you quite sure you are prepared for whatever shenanigans they have drawn you into?"

"Well, as we both know, Your Highness, youth can be so fleeting. I am honored that you and the princess deemed me worthy and capable of participating in hers."

Shuri could see Mother get flustered then. "What

are you getting into, child?" she asks the princess directly.

"Nothing at all for you to be concerned about, Mother. You chose Nakia to by my Msingi for good reason."

Once they finally make it out—T'Challa just so happened to call and request Mother's assistance with an urgent matter of diplomacy, and based on the wink Nakia tosses at Shuri when said call comes in, the princess presumes her Msingi may have had something to do with it—the trio of alien hunters and their trusty chaperone finally get underway.

To Shuri's delighted surprise, Nakia seems far more excited about the "grand adventure" than the princess would've expected. And while she, K'Marah, and Miles are filling Nakia in on the details of their bizarre quest—and Nakia gasps and whoops and fist-pumps (the Dora was especially impressed with the fake-gem tracker placement tactic)—Shuri expresses her astonishment over the Dora's enthusiasm.

"Are you kidding me? I *live* for this stuff!" Nakia replies. "Who do you think accompanied your brother in *his* heyday? I was *his* K'Marah!"

"Whoa. I never would've thought of that," Shuri says.

Nakia leans in. So they all do. "Stays between the

four of us, yes? But it was T'Challa's idea to assign *me* as your Msingi. He even overrode the queen. Which is an exceedingly rare thing for him to do, mind you. She wanted to assign a senior Dora named Kakhulu, and if she'd succeeded . . . well, this adventure certainly wouldn't be happening."

"Huh," Shuri replies.

"He really believes in you, T'Challa does," Nakia continues. "Now where exactly *is* this 'alien symbiote' we are after?"

"Ah, yes," Shuri says, gulping down the knot in her throat at Nakia's words about T'Challa's belief in her. "Based on his previous patterns of overnight movement and daytime stillness, we presume that the symbiote is currently at rest somewhere in the Jabari-Lands." She opens the tracking app on her Kimoyo card, and her eyes go wide. "Ahhh . . . One moment."

Which turns into two. Three. A full minute and thirty seconds. She deletes and reinstalls the app. Turns her Kimoyo card off, then back on. Refreshes over and over again . . .

"Everything cool, Shuri?" Miles says.

"Yeah. You're looking a little panicked, Princess," from K'Marah.

Shuri stares at the screen for a few more seconds, then sighs. "The tracker is . . ." She looks up at her friends and her Msingi, who all look like they're waiting to hear the results of some pivotal, globe-impacting election (not that there's ever *been* an election in Wakanda, but she's read about such things in her Global Diplomacy and World Governments course with her least favorite instructor, Scholar M'Walimu). "It's not picking up a signal," Shuri says, defeated. "I have no idea where he is."

"Oh," Miles says, clearly disappointed. "Okay."

"I think maybe the batteries in the tracking devices are becoming depleted," Shuri continues, desperate to come up with an explanation that doesn't involve the trackers being destroyed. "Which would mean the signal range has contracted."

"Ah, so if we get *closer* to devices, we will be able to pick up the signal?" Nakia asks.

"That is my prediction, yes."

"Wonderful. With that said, let us direct our course straight to the mountains."

◇◇◇◇◇

Except even near the mountains, there's no signal.

To avoid violating their countrymen's customs by entering Jabari airspace, the symbiote-seeking cohort can only circle the perimeter of the white-topped range, which stretches approximately 101 kilometers (or sixty-three miles for Miles) top to bottom and thirty-two kilometers (twenty or so miles) across. In other words, far too much terrain for them to wade into on foot without any notion of where the symbiote might be.

And yet they continue to circle the 221-kilometer perimeter. Hoping against hope that a signal will pop up, and distracting themselves with talks of potential plans for after they catch the symbiote they can't even locate.

At the two-hour mark, K'Marah gets visibly fidgety.

"Uhhh . . . you okay?" Miles asks.

She covers her face. "I have to go to the bathroom."

Secretly, Shuri is relieved, and she's fairly sure from the looks on Miles's and Nakia's faces that they are as well. A break from the monotony of mountain circling would likely be good for all parties.

"Oh!" Nakia says (quite cheerfully, mind you). "All right. If you consent, Your Majesty, my suggestion is that we pause our signal search for a bathroom break and some sustenance. Perhaps in the birth city of our very own General Okoye: Birnin Bashenga."

"Ooh, I've never been there!" K'Marah says.

"I haven't, either," Shuri replies, not realizing how bizarre a fact it is until the words are in the air. Never having visited other cities in a nation she is first in line to rule?

"Yes," Shuri says. "Let's go there."

◇◇◇◇◇

The first thing the princess notices once they step into the city limits: how much slower the pace of life seems to be.

"Well, this is different," Miles says. "Still *clearly* more advanced than where I come from . . ." He watches a hovercar zip by. "But different than the city where *you* all live."

"You can say that again," from K'Marah.

"You said that General Okoye was born here, Nakia?" Shuri asks, taking in the shorter, much less shiny buildings. Many seem to be made of concrete or stone. Miles is right: These are very much *not* the Vibranium-reinforced glass-and-steel skyscrapers that tower throughout the capital.

"Correct," Nakia replies. "Though it was a bit less city-like then."

"It feels so much older here," K'Marah says, looking around. "They *do* have flushing toilets, yes?"

This makes Miles laugh.

"K'Marah." The princess shakes her head.

"What? It's a valid question, is it not?"

"Yes, there are flushing toilets, Karami," Nakia says

with a grin. "And I believe there is a coffee shop up there on the left. We can all do our business, then catch a taxi-craft into the throbbing heart of the city."

As it turns out, *throbbing* is not an understatement. There is so much hustle and bustle and movement in Birnin Bashenga's center, the air truly feels as though it's beating to a rhythm. And K'Marah was right about the place feeling *older*. There's a stillness here—in spite of all the motion—that seems rooted in the long-established city.

They see a cluster of men beating on a stunning variety of ngoma drums, and a group of children playing hand-clap games. The air is thick with the mixed fragrance of fresh herbs and spices and cooking food, and the clothing worn by the "Bashengans," as Shuri heard them called, is intensely bright and wildly patterned. And a bit heavier than what is worn in Birnin Zana.

"It's chilly here!" K'Marah says, rubbing her arms.

"Oh yes," from Nakia. "The average temperatures are slightly lower than in the capital. Fewer buildings to trap the heat and all that."

"This place is dope, though," Miles says, spinning in awe. "Like, there's an open-air market?? My mom would lose her *mind* over all these fresh fruits and vegetables."

All around them, Bashengans are shopping, chattering happily, waving to one another, stopping whatever they're doing to talk . . . Shuri cannot deny that the small city is incredible.

"There is a man who makes the most delicious muchomo and gonja—that's roasted goat and plantains"—she winks at Miles—"at the opposite end of the market. Okoye introduced me to him when she first showed me around this place. And don't let his tent and grill cart fool you. The food he makes is . . ." She sighs and puts her hand over her heart. "Glory to Bast."

"Wait, did you say *cart*?" Miles asks.

"I did . . ."

"Yoooo, it's like the halal dudes back home! This is AMAZING!"

Shuri, K'Marah, and Nakia all laugh.

"We can fill our bellies there and then return to our mission, yes?" the elder Dora says.

"Sounds good to me!" Miles rubs his stomach.

And off they go.

There's a short line, but the closer they get to the front, the more Shuri's stomach rumbles.

"Or is that . . . her hip?"

"Oh!" she exclaims, realizing that her Kimoyo card is buzzing. Must be Mother "checking in."

Except . . . it's not.

Her eyes go wide. "Ummm . . . guys?"

K'Marah, Miles, and Nakia all turn to her. So she holds the device up where they can see it. "We have a signal."

"Oh my gods!" K'Marah says, clapping her hands over her mouth.

"Now we're talking," from Nakia.

"Where is he?" Miles says in a whisper. "Close by, I'm assuming?" He randomly looks down at his clothes: blue jeans, black T-shirt, and black-and-red hoodie.

A bit odd, but the princess has no time to think anything of it.

Quick as she can, Shuri pings their location. At first she doesn't see it in reference to those telltale three yellow dots . . . but then she zooms in. "He's, uhhhh . . . close," Shuri says, a slight quaver in her voice. "Like . . . very, *very* close."

"Mmmm . . . *how* close?" from K'Marah.

"Like fewer-than-one-hundred-meters-away close." She looks from her card to the right. The food cart is at the southern end of the open-air market, and then there's a street with hovercars traveling east and west. On the opposite side of the street there's a wide, three-story stone building.

"Huh," Nakia says. "That's the Bashengan Museum of Natural History and Artifacts."

"Yep," Shuri says. "Definitely where he is."

"But it's *daytime*!" K'Marah exclaims. "Isn't he supposed to be *resting*?"

"Uh-oh," Miles says.

K'Marah rounds on him. "What do you mean 'uh-oh'? What is *'uh-oh'*?"

"Well, if the symbiote is up and out during the day, it could only mean one thing."

"And what is that?" from Nakia, who is as calm as an undisturbed lake on a windless day.

"It means the host has become complicit," Miles explains. "Whomever the symbiote has inhabited is now working *with* him."

"Ah" is all Shuri can muster.

"And not to be, like, *alarmist* or whatever? But if K'Marah's theory is right and said host is a mutant . . . Well, that could mean a whole lotta *extra* trouble."

12

VENBANE

Shuri doesn't know how much time they have, or more important: what to actually *do*. This was supposed to be a pit stop, as she's heard it called. (Which has something to do with driving petrol-fueled cars around in circles at exceedingly high speeds. Westerners are so bizarre.) She has neither the sonic blaster they intend to use to try and force the symbiote to detach from the host, nor the host hexahedron to "catch" it, within any sort of reach.

But they also can't just . . . let him go. Well, if he's not gone already. The princess is 99.4 percent certain the nebular gem is not inside that museum.

She holds her breath and lifts her Kimoyo card to check and see if the signal is still there and . . .

It is. "Thank Bast," she says.

"For *what*, precisely? Delivering a signal when we are ill-prepared?" from K'Marah. (Who else?)

"Hush, Little Dora." Shuri's shoulders tense up, and she peeks around at the sky. "You mustn't speak ill of the Panther goddess."

"I must concur, beloved Karami," Nakia whispers.

"I am *thanking* her because, be it blessing or curse, our intruder has not moved. Which means that if we . . . What's that phrase, Miles? *Lay our cards left?*"

Miles snorts. "*Play our cards right,*" he says. "But close enough."

"Yes. That. If we play our cards right, we may be able to approach him and just . . . talk."

"And exactly what do you intend to say, Shuri? 'Come on back to our vessel and see the *box* we made for you! And if you climb inside, we can trap and keep you forever?'"

"You are being so *dramatic*, K'Marah!"

"*Realistic*, Shuri. I am being *realistic*. And trying to protect our lives!"

"Girls, girls," Nakia says. "Enough already."

Shuri checks the card again. Still there.

"Now, as I understand it, you have encountered the monster before," the elder Dora continues. "Yes?"

"Yes, but don't say the *m*-word to his face," Shuri says. "He is *not* a fan of being called a monster."

"Understood." Nakia looks at the museum and squints. "I can't believe I am asking this, but—" She turns back to Shuri and K'Marah. "Would you say he's *reasonable*?"

Shuri ponders for a moment. "I mean . . . yes? He obviously didn't hurt us. And he made it clear that all he wanted was the gem."

"All right. So with that in mind, do you think it plausible that we *could* talk to him?"

K'Marah throws her hands up. "You've all gone mad!"

"They actually have a point," Miles chimes in. "Especially if the host really *is* your . . . former homeboy, K'Marah. As I mentioned, the fact that he's out in the daytime means the host *knows* he's there and is, like, in cahoots with him. You said dude had been reaching out . . . We could totally use you as bait."

K'Marah reels back as though she's been punched (*dra-ma-tic*).

"And if nothing else, we can at least try and find

out *why* he's looking for this gem," Shuri says. "So perhaps we don't catch him . . . but we *do* acquire some useful information for when he *is* caught."

This is how K'Marah—who was *very* reluctant, but gives in when bribed with a subscription to some magazine called *Vogue*—winds up creeping along the backside of an unfamiliar building with right arm crossed over her chest and her hand on her shoulder so she can hear Shuri's commands through her Kimoyo bracelet.

"That's it," Shuri says, watching the Karami from her, Nakia's, and Miles's hiding spot behind a large, discarded display case. She switches apps on her Kimoyo card to take another look at a floor plan she found—which may or may not have involved hacking the museum security (and potentially also turning the alarms off). "About ten or so more meters ahead, there is a recessed exit door," she says into her wrist as she moves back to the tracker. "He seems to be tucked into the nook there."

"I just want you to know that I am *not* your number one fan right now, Princess," K'Marah replies through gritted teeth. "If you were attacked by a rogue rhinoceros or something, I would *not* stick my neck out to protect you."

"You'll forgive me later. You're almost there. Just

remember: Approach with kindness and caution. And don't disconnect this call. We need to hear what is happening."

"I bet you *do*."

Within half a minute, they see K'Marah stop and turn to face the building. Her shoulders rise and fall as she takes a deep breath. Then, "Ahh . . . excuse me?" Shuri, Nakia, and Miles hear from Shuri's bracelet. "Henny? I mean . . . Mr. Alien Guy? Is that you? It's me . . . K'Marah?"

Shuri and K'Marah have no idea what's happening *within* the little nook, but K'Marah flinches. To the point where Nakia and Miles both seem ready to leap into action (though what the relatively scrawny Brooklyn symbiote expert intends to do against what is clearly a stronger, faster opponent is beyond the princess). But then:

"K'Marah?" The gravelly (and downright *grating*) voice is faint, but they can all hear it. "You . . . girlfriend?"

"Yo, it *is* him!" Miles says. "She was right!"

Shuri is relieved, but also . . . "Oh dear *gods*, don't let her say anything offensive." She puts her head in her hands. "I can't even watch."

But K'Marah says, "Ahhh . . . at one point, yes? But just good friend now."

The being steps out of the nook, and Shuri and company all gasp.

K'Marah, however, doesn't move.

"That's my girl," Shuri whispers. "Rising to the challenge as per usual."

"Henbane say you *not* friend," the symbiote goes on.

Shuri's throat tightens. "Uh-oh . . ."

"Okay, that's true," K'Marah says.

"What is she *doing*?" from Miles. "You told her not to offend him!"

The Dora Karami continues: "I have not been a good friend as of late. But I would like to be now, if you will allow it." She drops her head and dips into a slight curtsy.

"Wow," from Nakia. "Way to sell it."

"My friends and I would like to . . . help you," K'Marah goes on.

"No 'friends.' Only ONE friend. Princess Shuri."

"Ah, yes! You would like to speak to the princess?"

"No like. But will."

(Shuri huffs. What does he mean, *no like*??)

"Okay," K'Marah says. "So if Shuri comes, you will speak with her?"

The symbiote nods once.

But Shuri doesn't move.

"Uhh, Princess?" Miles says. "I think that's your cue."

"Ah. Right."

Shuri steps out from the cozy safety of their hiding place, and makes her way toward K'Marah and her (certainly changed) ex-beau. She still remembers that awful, poisoned tracker bracelet he gave her for the sake of helping the evil giantess Zanda with her invasion mission. And how he decimated a swath of the Wakandan border forest that was ten kilometers long and eight meters wide. How he almost completely destroyed every single heart-shaped herb plant in the Sacred Field.

And T'Challa just . . . let him go. The princess has to temper her rage as she approaches. Probably an exceedingly good thing that all her weapons were left behind in the transport vessel.

Once she reaches K'Marah's side, Shuri forces a smile. "Lovely to see you again, Mr., ahhh—"

"Venbane," he replies.

"Huh?"

"Name *VENBANE* now!"

"All right," Shuri says. "Venbane."

"Gem not in museum," he says then. "You have gem. I no find in room, but you have. Give to me."

"Ahhh . . ." *Don't panic, don't panic.* "Are you sure you haven't confused *me* with a different princess? Maybeeee . . . Zanda? Of Narobia?"

"Big lady no have. Checked."

"Wait . . . so you *did* go to Narobia?"

"Big lady have gem last. I check big lady mind. See you. Now you have. Gem here. Venbane can feel. Give to Venbane."

"I, ummm . . ." *He came here because of Zanda?* "I seem to have misplaced it? Looking for it, though! Can you tell me . . . what you want to *do* with it?"

"We go home to Klyntar," he says. "Henbane come with—"

"Wait, *what*?" from K'Marah.

Shuri gives her a quick jab in her side with an elbow.

"Henbane will go home with you?"

"Yes. We Venbane now. Need gem. Go home. Gem from MY home. You give to Venbane."

"Absolutely!" Shuri replies.

"You no give to Venbane; Venbane call friends."

"It's yours; it's yours!" Shuri says. Clueless as to what that means, but with no interest in finding out. "One hundred and ten *percent* yours! Just as soon as I, ummm . . . remember where I put it!"

"Would you like to come back to the palace and help us look?" K'Marah blurts.

Shuri almost chokes on her tongue.

"You could RIDE with us inside our TRANSPORT VESSEL, and THE PRINCESS will show you what a HOSTING HEXA-whoodiewhatty looks like!" (*This girl is so awful at hint dropping,* Shuri thinks.)

Venbane's head drops to one side. "You take Venbane to palace?"

"Of course!" K'Marah says.

"You give Venbane tour?"

"Ehhhh . . . OW!" from Shuri. (Now K'Marah's the one throwing elbows.) "Yes, yes," Shuri says. "Definitely! No question at all!"

He seems to ponder this for a few moments before his giant white eyes narrow, making him appear *more* menacing—which Shuri didn't realize was possible. "This no trick?" he says. "You no trick Venbane. Trick bad idea."

"Oh . . . Venny!" K'Marah begins. "We would *nev*—"

But K'Marah doesn't get the rest out because the museum door opens, and a girl—likely around Miles's age—steps out.

Shuri steps forward with her hands raised, attempting to warn the girl not to scream . . . but it's too late. She lets it rip, and Shuri and K'Marah watch in a combination of awe and horror as Venbane claps his hands over the sides of his head and his entire body begins to vibrate so fast, his form blurs at the edges.

He thrashes and flails, but then he rounds on the girl. His razor-sharp, talon-like claws are now visible.

"NOOOO!" the princess shouts, lunging forward.

"SHURI, WAIT—!" But K'Marah reaches for her friend a hair too late.

When Venbane whips back around, the young royal has just stepped into the path of his moving arm. And then Shuri stands up straight, stock-still.

The other, older girl stops screaming and promptly faints.

"SHURI!" K'Marah shouts again, stepping forward to grab Shuri's shoulder.

The princess turns around, and K'Marah's hands fly to cover her mouth.

"Oh my gods! SHURI!"

"Venbane no mean!" The symbiote's voice sounds far off to the princess, though she could've sworn he was right behind her. "Mistake! Venbane no mean to hurt princess! Venbane—"

But that's all she hears. On instinct, she puts a hand to her midsection and discovers something warm and sticky that definitely wasn't there before.

At least she doesn't think it was . . .

Everything creeps black as her vision clouds.

No sight. No sound.

And then the princess is falling.

MISSION LOG

——TRANSMISSION INTERRUPTED——

13

HEALER

When Shuri comes to, she's covered in a pile of blankets so heavy, she can't lift her arms or legs. The princess opens her mouth to scream, but finds it so dry, she shuts it again out of fear that her tongue might crack and crumble to pieces.

Also quite dry are her eyes, but they do slowly adjust to the dim light. She turns her head to the left, and though pain, sharp and insistent, shoots down both arms into her fingertips, the princess is relieved to see warm light filtering through the wooden blind that's pulled low over the room's lone window.

Where is she? And where is everyone else?

She shuts her eyes and groans.

"Oh, beloved Bast!" comes a familiar voice from somewhere in the room. "I think she's waking up!"

When Shuri next opens her eyes, there are two silhouettes looming above her: a girl with a round face and elaborate braided hairdo, and a boy with hair that is higher at the top than on the sides. "Oh my gods, Shuri, oh my gods!" the girl says, throwing herself onto the princess's upper half.

"Owwwww," the young royal manages to croak. *Why does her body ache so badly?*

"Sorry, sorry!" the little Dora replies. "I am just so happy that you are *alive*."

The boy makes that "teeth-sucking" sound Shuri has seen American teenagers make on television shows when they don't like something said by an adult. "We knew she wasn't gonna *die*, K'Marah. Miss Umela told us that much—"

"Yes, well, she could've been *wrong*, couldn't she?"

"Dramatic," Shuri forces up from her dry throat and through her cracked lips.

"Oh, shut up," K'Marah replies. "Without my *drama*, as you call it, we wouldn't have gotten you here."

"You can say that again," Miles groans.

"What . . ." Shuri says (not even the pain of

speaking in her current state could temper the princess's need to know things). "What do you mean?"

"Well, when you went down, your friend here went tearing through the marketplace, shouting 'Someone! Anyone! Your most high Majesty, Princess Shuri, needs a healer! Help, or you will all be vanquished and/or banished!'" The high-pitched voice Miles uses to mimic K'Marah makes Shuri want to laugh, but she fights it because: pain. Much, much pain.

"I do *not* sound that way," K'Marah huffs.

Oh, you most certainly do, Shuri wants to add, but can't.

"You actually do sometimes, Karami," cuts in a third voice. Light floods the room as the blind is lifted. "Your Majesty, how are you feeling?"

When Nakia's face appears above the princess, she almost bursts into tears. The sight of her Msingi fills Shuri with so much unexpected emotion, she can't figure out what she's actually feeling.

"You took quite a blow," the elder Dora continues.

Shuri opens her mouth to speak again. "Wha—"

But it hurts too much.

"Ah yes," Nakia says. "Umela warned us of this. Hold tight, eh?" (As though there's anything *else* she could do?)

Miles looks to his left—presumably to make sure

Nakia is gone?—before he leans in closer. "Yo, not to freak you out? But that was one of the wildest things I've ever seen," he says in a near whisper. "And I've seen a *lot* of wild things. Like . . ." He shakes his head. "Just trust me. But *that* . . . The way the area around the gashes immediately, like, turned black and wrinkly, and these little yellow *flowers* started poppin' up in the wounds—"

"I believe that's quite enough, young Mr. Morales," Nakia says as she returns. But Miles's statement about little yellow flowers has already taken root in Shuri's head. A pair of images pops into her mind: one of blackened and decayed security forest tree trunks, and the other of a wide swath of shriveled heart-shaped herb plants—both of which were covered in little yellow flowers.

A sign that Henbane's mutant toxin was at work.

Had it gotten *inside* Shuri's body?

"Princess, this is Mganga Umela," Nakia says, pulling the princess from her ponderings. She gestures to a beautiful—and remarkably regal—dark brown–skinned woman who has come into Shuri's view.

"An honor, Your Majesty," she says with a slight bow. (*How do Mother and T'Challa deal with everyone* bowing *to them all the time?* Shuri wonders.)

"K'Marah, Miles, if you will, please," Nakia says.

Shuri's friends disappear from her bedside, and the woman, Mganga Umela, takes their place. "You may call me Umela," she says, beginning to remove Shuri's coverings one by one. The lifted weight is great, but the ache that floods her limbs in place of the pressure? Not so much.

Umela seems to read Shuri's mind. "I presume you are in quite a bit of pain," she says. "The toxin that entered your bloodstream was incredibly potent. I had to use a powerful—and atypical—combination of herbs and tinctures to flush it out."

Once Umela has removed the final blanket, she disappears from view, and Shuri can hear the sound of things being picked up and put down, and the clanking of glass that the princess has no doubt means something is being stirred. (A scientist always knows.) Then Umela returns and kneels beside her. She lifts the left side of the top Shuri is wearing (which feels much looser than any she would typically put on), and then there's the sharp bite of sticky bandage adhesive being removed from the skin. "Ah, that's looking better!" Umela says.

"Yeah, cuz there's no *flowers* growing out her stomach—"

"*Miles!*" K'Marah barks. "Zip it!"

Umela grins and shakes her head. "This is definitely

going to sting, Your Highness," she says. "But you'll thank me once it subsides. Ready?"

Shuri nods . . . and instantly regrets it. Because whatever this Umela woman is spreading over her abdomen might as well be made of the blue fire from an oxyacetylene torch. The burn slithers beneath her skin and travels through *every* inch of her body.

She couldn't scream if she wanted to. (And she certainly wants to.)

But then . . . a cooling sensation follows the same course. And once the strange feeling diminishes, so do all of Shuri's aches and pains.

She has a frightening flash of memory: her hand against her belly, and something warm and wet that shouldn't have been there. *Blood,* she realizes. On instinct, she touches the exact same spot: There are four slightly raised lines—that she's *certain* weren't there before—and her skin is cold to the touch, but it's definitely *closed* now.

"Lift your head," Umela says.

When she complies, the beautiful woman places a small bowl to Shuri's lips and tips it so that a cold, viscous liquid spills into the princess's mouth. The flavor reminds her of fresh passion fruit nectar.

And as it travels down her throat, her limbs take on a lightness that wasn't there.

"Do you think you can sit up?" Umela says.

Shuri ponders for a moment; then her muscles start to tingle, like they're just *dying* to be used. So she pops right up and swings her legs over the edge of the bed she's on. It's higher than she anticipated, but no matter: She hops off and lands on her feet with no problem or pain.

"Great Bast!" Shuri shakes out her arms and legs, and commences bouncing on her toes. "I haven't felt this energized since . . . I don't think I've *ever* felt this energized."

Umela chuckles. "Excellent," she says with a nod. Shuri watches her cross the room—a much smaller space than she realized—to return her implements to a little round table situated beside a cabinet full of different bottles and vials and jars of various sizes and colors. That's when Shuri notices the symbol carved into the dirt wall above the window. Three stacked wavy lines centered inside an eight-rayed sun.

It matches the tattoo on the back of Umela's right hand.

The princess gasps. "You're an Asili!" she says. The princess learned about the ancient clan of Wakandans—said to be born with the power of healing in the tips of their fingers—while studying *The Medicinal Practices of East Africa* in her Afro-Biology class. Shuri was vaguely convinced that their existence was myth. And yet:

"The only one in the region, yes," Umela says. "But we can talk about that more on the way."

Shuri's eyebrows rise. "Are we going somewhere?"

"Sure are, Princess," K'Marah says. "Especially now that we know you're not dead."

"K'Marah." Nakia puts a hand on her forehead.

"Miss Umela here is going to show us the way!" Miles says, so excited he's practically leaping out of his typical-American-teenager getup.

Very cute, this Miles Morales. "The way to where?" Shuri says, doing her best to focus. Her body is good as new, but there's clearly still a bit of a fog over her mind.

"Into the Jabari-Lands," Umela says, pulling open a door so well blended into the wall, Shuri hadn't noticed it. She produces four sets of hooded white coveralls and hands them to each member of the princess's entourage.

"We watched Venbane flee into the mountains," K'Marah says. "And while you were clomping around at death's doorstep, we decided that if you ever came back—"

"*When* you woke up," Miles corrects. He shakes his head.

"If, when. Gonja, maduro . . ." The little Dora waves the differences off. "We are going to the main Jabari village to see if anyone knows where Henbane is."

"We have a three-hour trek through the Crystal Forest," Umela says. "Put on the coveralls and you'll stay warm."

Everyone complies, and once Shuri has hers buttoned up, she suddenly feels as though she is wrapped in the softest, coziest blanket known to mankind.

"Whoa!" she says, lifting her arms to examine the fabric. "What on earth are these made of?"

"Ancient secret," Umela says with a wink. "Now come on. Our chariot awaits."

14

JOURNEY

Once they are out of the kibanda, as Umela refers to the hut, and Shuri has a chance to look around, she is surprised at their location. To the left, in the near distance, the princess can see a trio of exceedingly tall, slant-top buildings. Those are found only in one place within all of Wakanda: Birnan T'Chaka. The city named for Baba.

To the right: the foot of the mountains.

This is as close as she's ever been to the Jabari-Lands.

After a trip to the *Predator* to retrieve the sound

devices and catching cube, they prepare to depart. As it turns out, the "chariot" is a wooden carriage attached to a very large buffalo. Shuri doesn't think she's ever seen a mode of transportation this primitive. (*Will it fall apart on bumpy terrain?*)

Also, the massive, horned creature does not look friendly. "Uhhhh—"

"She won't hurt you, Your Majesty," Umela says, rubbing the creature above its front right leg. "She is a laini buffalo. Like our border tribe's rhinoceroses, and the white gorillas we're likely to see in the forest, her species is found only here in Wakanda. This lady's breed developed some unique characteristics—likely from feeding on grasses grown in soil laced with Vibranium, as all the soil is here. As you can see, she's approximately one-and-a-half times the size of a typical African buffalo, and she has capability of climate adaptation."

K'Marah cuts in. "Ummm . . . no offense, Umela, but right now you're speaking a dialect called *Shuri*, and none of the rest of us can understand."

"Oh, will you *hush*?" Shuri replies.

Nakia and Umela shake their heads in tandem. "I don't know how you do it, Naki," Umela says.

"Oh, trust me, Sister: I haven't the vaguest idea, either," Nakia replies.

"Wait, you two are *sisters*?" Miles asks.

Nakia lifts a hand. "We can get into that on the way. You were saying, Umi?"

"Thank you, Naki." Umela turns to K'Marah. "What I mean is that this species of buffalo can thrive in any climate. Their bodies adapt to changes in temperature almost instantly."

"Ah," K'Marah says. "Understood. *And* pretty cool. Or warm!"

"Bast help me," Shuri says.

Miles leans in and lowers his voice: "Back home, we call that a 'dad joke.'"

"The four of you may climb into the carriage," Umela says. "I will guide us from my perch on Mumu's back."

They climb in and each take a seat on one of the two wooden benches jutting out of the front and back walls.

"Well, *this* should be interesting," K'Marah says. "Though potentially uncomfortable."

"Did she say *Mumu*?" from Miles.

The carriage jerks, and they're off.

As they journey, bits and pieces from the twenty-four hours that the princess missed come together (she almost chokes when they reveal that she was out for that long). She'd been scratched by "Venbane," as he calls himself now, and Miles had been right: an alien symbiote with *extremely* sharp claws bonded with a mutant whose power is poison? Definitely a dangerous combination.

K'Marah is convinced that he wasn't trying to hurt Shuri, though Miles isn't so sure. "I've, uhh . . . *experienced* some terrible things interacting with Venom," he says. "While I'm sure not *all* symbiotes are bad, I'm also sure that taking out a princess who won't give one what he wants wouldn't be out of character."

Shuri also learns that it's a miracle that she's even here. "Umela was saying that although you would definitely survive, the amount of poison in your system would've killed anyone *but* you," Nakia says. "She thinks you might have heightened levels of immunity and faster cell turnover as a result of being a direct descendant of Bashenga."

"Is . . . that possible?" Shuri asks, stunned. And a bit uncomfortable for some reason.

Nakia shrugs. "I don't see why not."

Which is when they get into Nakia's background, connection to Umela, and how they even got to where they were when Shuri woke up: "Umi is my adoptive elder sister. In fact, this was a point on which your brother and I were able to connect as youngsters: being the first*born* but second child."

"That's kinda wild," Miles chimes in.

Nakia smiles. "We were raised in a small fishing village some fifty kilometers southeast of Umi's kibanda, right between Birnin Bashenga and Birnin Djata."

"So basically: Ya girl over here"—he cuts his gaze at K'Marah, and Shuri gets an instant understanding of the term *side-eye*—"went ripping through that dope little city we were in, threatening people left and right on *your* behalf until Nakia managed to get her attention and let her know *we* could take her to a healer." He shakes his head.

"I was concerned for my best friend's *life*, thank you very much, Mr. New York City."

"I'm from *Brooklyn*. Get it right, warrior girl."

"Whatever." K'Marah sticks her chin in the air in defiance, and crosses her arms.

"They've been bickering like this since yesterday," Nakia says with a shake of her head. "LONG story short," she continues, "we got you to my sister, and here we are: officially en route to our intended destination. With *some* idea of what we are up against and why. Glory to Bast."

"Okay, but . . ." Shuri's not exactly sure how to phrase the question. Hopefully it doesn't come across disrespectfully . . . "Why does your sister know how to get to the Jabari village? Aren't they unwelcoming of outsiders?"

"Well, according to what she told *me* when I asked that precise question, if that 'outsider' has a gift of healing, and you are part of a people group that eschews any use of modern medicine . . ."

"Wait, so she's like the Jabari's *doctor*?" K'Marah asks.

Nakia shrugs. "That's one way to look at it."

"Wild," K'Marah says, clearly influenced by Miles's way of speaking.

The four of them lapse into silence.

After a few minutes, the carriage goes over a large bump, and all four of its passengers get bounced from their seats.

"Sorry!" they hear Umela shout from outside. "Terrain here's a little—"

There's a loud *THUMP* on the roof, and the entire carriage rocks side to side.

Shuri looks out the small window opposite the door. "What on earth was tha—"

The carriage bounces again.

They all sit in stunned silence until there's a loud *CRACK* outside the carriage. "BACK, YOU BEAST!" Umela bellows before there's a second, even louder *CRACK*.

And then comes a roar that makes the wooden box they're in literally tremble on its wheels.

"Yeah, *not* okay," Nakia says, unzipping her coveralls, and pulling her collapsed spear from its hidden holster beneath the front panel of her Dora uniform. And before Shuri can object, her Msingi has shed the warm jumpsuit all together and is exiting the carriage. "Get away from my sister, ape!" they hear her yell.

Something smacks into the carriage's side, and the trio is tossed against the inner wall.

"Uhhh, no idea what the heck is going on out there," Miles says, climbing out of his heatsuit. "But I, uhh . . ." He looks back and forth between the girls. "Uhhh . . . yeah." Then he's out as well.

Shuri shakes her head. "Of course an American boy whose expertise is alien symbiotes would flee at the first sign of—"

There's another *THUMP*, and the rickety carriage rocks again.

The girls stare at each other for moment, understanding passing between them without either saying a word.

Then they're both shedding their heated jumpsuits and climbing out, too.

What they see once their feet hit the ground is so far beyond what the princess is expecting, she freezes in place: There, on the path not ten meters in front of Mumu—who appears completely unfazed—Umela and Nakia are trying to subdue a white gorilla the size of a Wakandan border rhino (that is, *gigantic*). With *very* sharp fangs. Which Shuri sees when the creature roars in frustration as Umela gets her whip wrapped around its hind legs. She pulls at the same time Nakia does a (very impressive) front flip and kicks the gorilla right in the chest. It topples backward, landing with a crash that makes the snow-dusted trees quiver.

"Bast, Kokou, *and* Nyami," K'Marah breathes beside the princess.

"You forgot Thoth, Mujaji, and Ptah," Shuri replies. "Might as well call on *all* the Orisha. We clearly need it."

"So what do we do?"

As if in answer, Nakia's head whips around. "STAY BACK, GIRLS!" she commands.

And then the strangest thing happens: Something *SWOOPS* over the girls' heads and shoots a white object at the gorilla before disappearing back into the trees. The creature howls and reaches for its face . . . Which is when another shot of something white hits the creature. And appears to glue its hands over its eyes.

"What the—" K'Marah begins, snatching the words right out of Shuri's brain.

Both girls look up into the trees . . . and see nothing.

"Almost got him!" Umela says, pulling the girls' attention back to the increasingly bizarre scene before them. The Asili pulls something from the pocket of her coveralls—she's the only person still wearing them—and jabs it into the gorilla's right side.

The creature immediately stops thrashing and goes limp.

"Whew!" Umela stands upright and wipes her brow with the back of her hand. Then after giving the massive animal a shove with the toe of her boot to make sure it's really knocked out, she approaches its head and squats down to look at the substance coating the creature's face.

Shuri and K'Marah look at each other and then jog over.

"What is it?" they hear Nakia say to Umela. "And where did it come from?"

"No idea of the origin. But it looks like . . . some sort of webbing?"

"What'd I miss?" comes Miles's voice from behind them.

All four Wakandans jump.

"Where on earth did you *go*?" Shuri says.

"Oh. Uhhhh . . . I don't really do giant, scary animals that could eat me?" he answers, with a shrug that's more nonchalant than the princess would expect.

"Really now?" K'Marah says. Shuri braces herself for the tongue-lashing headed Miles's way from the little Dora . . .

But it doesn't come. In fact, K'Marah just looks the boy over and narrows her eyes. "Your jacket is inside out" is all she says.

"Oh snap," Miles begins, stretching his arms out—

There's another roar.

Answered by another one.

Then by a third. And another.

One by one, four giant white gorillas stalk out of the trees and move in on them.

"Ummmmm . . ." Miles says. "That's . . . not good?"

"Are you *asking* or making an assertion?" Shuri says as she and K'Marah get back-to-back. "Because there's really no *question*, in my humble opinion!"

Nakia and Umela join the trio, and they form a tight circle with everyone facing out. The Wakandans all have weapons drawn.

Not that they'd do any good against this many rhino-size primates. "Nakia!" K'Marah hisses. "You didn't train me for this!"

The gorillas get closer.

"What do we do, what do we do?" Shuri says.

"Brace ourselves for what will hopefully be a quick, and therefore painless, death!" K'Marah replies.

"Not exactly helpful, Karami," Nakia says, chill as ever. (*How does she manage to remain so* calm?)

"I've never seen this many at once before," Umela says.

"Can we run?" from Miles. (Of course.)

"We wouldn't get far," Umela replies. "They are swifter than their size would suggest."

"So does that mean . . . ?" Shuri begins, but can't bring herself to go on: *We're doomed?*

A fifth roar rips through the air. Much louder and . . . angrier than the others.

In fact, even *they* take notice. All four of the present beasts stand upright, almost at attention.

"Oh, thank Bast," Umela says, releasing an exhale they all can feel.

Again, K'Marah snatches a thought right from Shuri's mind: "Doesn't a fifth one mean *more* trouble?"

"You'll see," Umela replies. "You can lower your weapons."

"Mmmm . . . no disrespect, beloved Asili, but I'm not sure that's entirely wise—"

The rest of the statement dies on Shuri's tongue.

Because out from among the trees steps not a fifth white gorilla, but a person wearing what looks like a suit made from the hide of one of the terrifying animals.

The man roars again—shockingly loud. Shuri's hands go immediately over her ears.

And then her mouth falls open. Because the gorillas all retreat.

"Wha—how??" K'Marah says at the same time Miles says, "Who is *that*?"

The man approaches them and lowers his gorilla-head hood (*gross*).

Shuri couldn't speak if she tried: He looks even *less* friendly than the beasts did.

Umela steps forward and bows. So Shuri and crew, Nakia included, do the same.

"M'Baku," Umela says. "Just the man we're looking for."

15

JABARI

After putting their warmth suits back on, Shuri grabs her backpack, and she and company continue their journey on foot. M'Baku, the very well-known and semi-notorious tribal leader—who Shuri has the urge to refer to as *Mr. Jabari Big Man, Sir*—leads Mumu along the path. And though a man of few words, he assures Umela that her carriage will be at her kibanda when she returns.

As it turns out, they were fairly close to the southern border of the Jabari-Lands. The entrance is through a mountain cave passageway flanked by a pair of large carved white gorillas. They look so real from a short distance away, Shuri can see why no one just struts up and waltzes on through.

What they see when they *exit* the tunnel takes Shuri's breath away.

Not only does the path lead into a full-blown city—with buildings not as tall as the ones in the capital, but certainly tall enough—on the way in they pass by acre after acre of lush farmland. Tomatoes, cabbage, broccoli, spinach, kale, peas, and maize. Beyond it on both sides are perfectly aligned rows of green that appear to be groves of fruit-bearing trees: apple, orange, plum, pear, peach, passion fruit. Shuri can also make out both banana and pineapple orchards, date palms, and a grapevine . . .

But the most astonishing thing is the rather beautiful layer of frost clinging to every speck of green in sight. It sparkles in the sun as they continue up the path.

"But how—" Shuri marvels as she looks around. "This shouldn't be *possible*! These crops can't grow in this climate!"

"Oh, they very well can," Umela says. "Vibranium-laced soil makes a number of seemingly impossible adaptations a reality."

"Oh, it's just like your buffalo!" Miles says, putting two and two together.

"Precisely."

Once they cross over a swiftly flowing stream and walk into the actual city, the princess's awe expands. There are paved streets just like the ones in Birnin Zana, though they're made for feet, not vehicles. The tall buildings are all made of stone—likely hewn from the surrounding mountains if the color is any indication. And the hustle and bustle of people moving in and out of them blows the princess's mind. "What do they do inside of *those*?" she asks Umela.

The response comes from the terrifying man—still in his gorilla suit—leading the way. "They live," he says in a tone that definitely has a *duh, dummy* ring to it.

Shuri decides not to ask any more questions.

The Jabari people themselves are nothing short of stunning. They wear far more clothing than Wakandans who live in the cities and villages across the plain—thick white fur–lined vests and coats, skirts and trousers that appear to be made from various animal pelts, and heavy fur-accented boots. Many of the adults have elaborate shoulder dressings and beautifully carved chest plates made of wood. But every Jabari Shuri has the pleasure of laying eyes on is some shade of deep brown, with both eyes and a smile that seem to sparkle in the sun.

"This is certainly not what I was expecting," K'Marah whispers to the princess.

"Me, either," Shuri replies.

As they continue their walk through the city center, Shuri can't help but wonder *why* she is so surprised by the beauty of the Jabari-Lands and tribespeople. No, she hasn't seen a single motorized, machinated, or electrified object, but the residents here are thriving.

Any reason why they wouldn't be?

The group continues straight through to the opposite end of the city and out the other end. After M'Baku sends Mumu off to graze in a small pasture that Shuri realizes is full of buffalo, they hang a left into a narrow valley between two towering cliffs. Every person who passes them going in the opposite direction crosses an arm over their chest and nods at M'Baku. Most of the time, he makes no acknowledgment at all, but occasionally he'll grunt in someone's direction. (While the Jabari aren't primitive by any stretch of the imagination, Mother would be appalled at their leader's utter lack of decorum.)

"This guy seems to be a pretty big deal," Miles says.

"He is the leader of this tribe," Shuri replies. "And though this is my first time actually encountering him, his strong-silent-type reputation preceded him well."

"M'Baku is a man of few words, yes," comes

Nakia's voice from behind them. "But he is well respected throughout our kingdom, and as you can see, he takes excellent care of his people. Now, both of you, zip it. We are here as friends of Umela, so if any of us bring offense, it will reflect poorly on *her* and jeopardize relationships she has taken years and years to cultivate."

"Ah," K'Marah says, and then she looks over her shoulder. "Duly noted, Msingi of Princess Shuri."

"Keep teasing me, and you shall come to regret it, Karami. Let's not forget that *I'm* the one who taught you most of your combat skills."

Then from Miles: *"Got 'em!"*

"Oh, you stay out of this, American boy," K'Marah grumbles.

They traverse the remainder of the long and winding trail in silence, barring an occasional gasp when they encounter something amazing. Like the stone bridge that crosses over a beautiful hot spring filled with smiling and laughing Jabari people, all heavy coats and boots cast aside on the surrounding rocks. Or the settlement they pass that's built beneath a high, curved cliff.

It's when they step into the clearing in front of their destination that the princess and her cohorts stop dead. Because the palace-style facade—complete with tall pillars and high arches and two towers topped with giant braziers full of crackling fire—is just that: a facade. It's all just carved into the face of a mountain.

"It's like that place in Jordan!" Miles says. "Petra, I think it's called? I saw it in this old movie my dad made me watch about this white dude named Indiana Jones."

At this, M'Baku slowly turns around. "And where do you think the Nabateans got the idea?" he asks.

No one responds.

They continue through the door-shaped opening in the rock and find themselves inside a cave-like space lit with torches. M'Baku pulls one from its wall sconce, and they continue forward, around a bend, along a steep incline, and then up a *looooong*, curved stone staircase.

And when they step into the space above?

"My. Gods," K'Marah breathes.

"You can say that again," from Miles. "I don't think I've ever seen anything this beautiful."

The space is shockingly similar to the palace's throne room. A perfectly centered throne decorated with all manner of animal hides and furs—fit for a king, for sure—surrounded by smaller but no less extravagant high-backed chairs. And the view *behind* the seats is absolutely breathtaking: They can see a huge, white-topped swath of the mountain range, and then much of the plain, city, stream, and glistening produce fields beyond.

At first Shuri wonders where the glass came from—there was none in any of the buildings they passed on the way in—but then it hits her: "Is that *ice*?" she says, stepping forward for another look.

M'Baku drops down into the center chair (of course). "Whatever else would it be, Your Majesty?"

Shuri's eyes go wide. "You know who I *am*?"

M'Baku glares at her (and she swears her soul shrinks two sizes), then bursts into booming laughter.

"M'Baku, be *nice*," Umela says, though she's grinning, too.

"Why are you here, Princess Shuri?" M'Baku asks. "I am certain that your mother and brother would be most vexed if they knew, eh?"

Shuri's eyes drop to her feet.

"Lift your head, girl. You are royalty. Descended from Bashenga," M'Baku barks. "This is your nation. Greet me with the confidence of your station."

Nakia clears her throat beside the princess as if to concur.

So Shuri picks up her chin, swallows, and speaks: "Greetings, Mr. M'Baku."

He smirks, but Shuri tries not to let it throw her off again.

"My companions and I have come in search of a Narobian boy taken into Jabari care some time ago."

A smile splits M'Baku's face. So bright, Shuri is almost knocked back by the sight of it.

"HENBANE!" he rumbles. "My, do I love that boy. Though I do not suggest permitting him to touch your plants. A *black* thumb that one has." He shakes his head.

"That's one way to describe it . . ." K'Marah says under her breath.

M'Baku turns serious again. "What do you want with him?" (*Did someone say* mood swings??)

At this, the backpack on Shuri's back seems to get heavier. It was bad enough sneaking the sonic blaster, sound cannon (for backup), CatEyez, and host hexahedron into this anti-tech establishment. Knowing she intends to use it on a boy the Jabari leader clearly favors? Absolutely terrifying. "Ahhhh, just to talk, really. We have a question about . . . Narobian politics." Of course, none of them expected to go through the *leader* of the Jabari to get to Henbane, so no one is prepared for this question. "My friend K'Marah here knows him—"

"How?"

And from the look on M'Baku's face, Shuri knows *not* to mention that "Henny" communicated with K'Marah electronically for weeks before they discovered his hand in Zanda's plot. Though she also can't figure out *how* he did; her Kimoyo card hasn't had a signal since they reached the mouth of the tunnel to the city. "Ah, you know. That whole herb thing? K'Marah's the one who, ahhh . . . talked him out of killing the final one!"

One of M'Baku's brows lift, but he doesn't press any further. Just shouts, "N'YOTA! COME!"

A boy no older than Miles in the face, but a head taller and significantly more muscular, strides into the room. (Which is when Shuri notices there's a corridor that probably leads to another gorgeous view from within this ice castle.) "Yes, Baba?" the boy says, reverently dipping his head.

Father??

"Escort these flatlanders to Henbane's hollow."

"Yes, Baba." The (very tall, fairly wide) boy turns to head down the stairs, and Shuri and crew all follow.

"Oh, and, Princess?"

Shuri resists the urge to pretend she didn't hear him and turns around. "Yes?"

"Tell my dear friend T'Challa that I said hello. And perhaps I will see him on Challenge Day next year."

◇◇◇◇◇

Shuri worries over M'Baku's final words to her the whole way to where Henbane lives. Though when they arrive, she sees that *hollow* is an apt descriptor: The place the Jabari leader's son led them to appears to be little more than a mountain cave.

At least from the outside.

"Here you are," the large boy says. "Henbane's hollow. He has been sleeping during the daytime a fair amount recently, but if you knock on the door hard enough, it should wake him." He turns to leave.

"Wait!" Shuri says. "Where are you going?"

"Back to my daily duties," he replies. "Henbane can get you back to the cliff path. Asili Umela knows the way from there." He smiles and nods at Nakia's big sis, and the woman nods back.

And then he's gone.

"Welp," K'Marah says. "Let's get this over with, shall we? Blowing and catching tools are at the ready?"

"*Shhh*, K'Marah!" Shuri looks around. "We're not supposed to have this stuff here, remember?" She takes a deep breath.

"I'll go in first," Miles says, surprising them all.

Shuri and K'Marah look at each other, both likely remembering the way he fled at the most recent sign of danger.

"Ummm . . . that's okay," the princess says. "K'Marah, will lead the way in and be the knocker."

"What?! Again??"

"Of course, again, K'Marah. You're the one he *knows*?" Shuri says. "And seems to trust."

"Umela and I will hang back here unless you call for us," Nakia says.

"Cool. So let's do this," from Miles.

"Easy for you to say, *Brooklyn* boy! No one is telling *you* to throw yourself on yet another sword!"

"Hey, I offered. But the princess has spoken—"

"Will you three get on with it already?" Umela says. "I am telling you, Sister: I could *not* do it."

"Fine." And K'Marah ducks beneath the low, rounded entrance and disappears into the dim space.

Miles and Shuri follow suit.

The cavern beyond is far bigger and taller than Shuri presumed. So tall, in fact, she can't see the ceiling.

Thankfully, the light filtering in through the cavern opening is bright enough for them to see the little wooden door set into the wall of rock in front of them.

"You know, Princess, this sort of reminds me of the entrance to your laboratory," K'Marah says. "The whole creepy cave that leads to a mysterious and out-of-place door. This motif must be *in* among you weirdos."

"Will you just zip it and knock?"

K'Marah chuckles but then does as she's asked. *Knock, knock, knock . . .*

They wait.

No answer.

K'Marah knocks harder: *KNOCK, KNOCK, KNOCK.*

Same thing.

"Maybe he's not here," Miles says. "We *did* see him out in the daytime a couple of days—"

"Do *not* finish that sentence," K'Marah says, rounding to point at Miles. "We have traveled too far in the frigid cold." She rotates back to the door and pounds it with her fist. *BAM, BAM, BAM.* "We almost got *eaten* by giant white gorillas . . ." *BAM, BAM, BAM.* "YOU, Princess, almost DIED . . ." *BAM, BAM, BAM.* "Hennyyyy! It's your favorite! I've come to see you! HENNYYYYY!"

"K'Marah, I don't think—"

"Wait . . ." Miles puts a hand up.

The hairs on Shuri's arms stand at attention. Something's not right. She looks at Miles, whose eyes are narrowed—but then suddenly widen. "K'Marah, DUCK!" he shouts before tackling Shuri to the ground.

"Hey! What giv—"

But she doesn't get the rest of the word out. Because just as K'Marah drops to the ground, something zips through the air over their heads and lands on the door.

Right where K'Marah had been standing.

"K'Marah, MOVE!" Miles shouts again.

The little Dora does, and not a moment after, the door flies from the hinges. Shuri and Miles both barely manage to roll out of the way as it comes at them.

Which is when Shuri realizes what the substance is. "Is that *webbing*?"

"Sure is," Miles says. He leaps to his feet. "It's time to catch a poisonous spider."

And then he jumps right out of his warmth suit.

16

CAPTURE

At first, the princess has *no* idea what's happening.

"Did you *see* that?" she says to K'Marah while gaping at the pile of crumpled white fabric on the cavern floor. "Where did he go?!"

K'Marah doesn't respond, too busy staring up into the darkness with a furrowed brow.

"K'Marah, did you—"

"Make sure he can't get out!" Miles's voice rings down from somewhere above them.

"Huh" is all Little Dora says.

"Did you hear me, Shuri?" Miles again. "Ahhh!

Tell Nakia and Umela to block the entrance!"

Not knowing what else to do, Shuri complies: "Uhhh . . . Umela! Nakia! Keep the cave entrance guarded!" she shouts in the direction of their only way out. "We found him!"

Whether or not they hear her, Shuri doesn't know. What *she* hears is grunting and shouting and an occasional bizarre *FWIP FWIP* sound.

"Get back here!" she hears Miles say. Then there's a *FWISH FWISH*, followed by a growl that lets Shuri know that the symbiote is not happy.

"Shuri!" K'Marah hisses. "In here!"

The princess scurries in the direction of the now-open doorway to the interior of Henbane's hollow. A warm yellow light emanates from inside, but it's not bright enough to illuminate the cave.

Then Shuri remembers. "K'Marah!" she says, stopping a few meters from the doorway. "I totally brought CatEyez for both of us—"

"But can you come *through* the doorway before telling—"

Venbane swings right in front of the princess, immediately followed by someone cloaked in all black with something red on its chest.

"WHOA!"

"Yeah, don't mind me!" Miles says from somewhere

above Shuri's head. "OWW! Uncalled for, you jerk!"

"Oh my gods! Miles, are you all right?" Shuri shouts. "Where even *are* you?"

"I'll be *much* better once you get that whole *blowing* and *catching* thing under way! Think you could speed that part up a bit? Man, how is this webbing so *strong*?"

Shuri crosses into the light but almost falls back when she sees what's on the other side. It's a living space, yes. Ringed with torches tucked into sconces around the space. There's a table and chairs, a sofa, a cabinet for kitchen implements, and a waist-high chest made of ice, full of blurred objects Shuri assumes are perishable foods. There's also a second wooden door that she assumes leads to some sort of sleeping quarters (is there a bathroom in there?). But the most astonishing things are the plants. Various shapes, sizes, and shades of green, very much alive.

And thriving.

"Yeah, I was shocked, too," K'Marah says, following Shuri's gaze around the room. "But no time to ponder over it now. We have to get this done before my alien-posessed ex-boyfriend eats my crush." She shakes her head. "How is any of this *real*?"

Shuri lowers her bag and yanks it open. "Here," she says, handing K'Marah a pair of the *very* high-tech glasses—and feeling bad anew for violating the Jabari no-tech rule. "Can't connect to any networks, so you'll have to manually turn on the scotopic-mode."

"The *what*?"

"Night vision, K'Marah. Even though technically it should be *dark* vision since it's not actually night—"

"Just tell me how to do it, Shuri!" K'Marah bellows.

"Oh, right." And Shuri complies.

Once their special glasses are settled, the princess passes K'Marah the sonic blaster—which is shaped like a small "bullhorn," as Shuri saw the funnel-shaped things called when building her prototype. Except *hers* doesn't make a loud, annoying sound.

What Shuri's does: emit ultrasonic waves—far too high-pitched for most *humans* to hear, but at a frequency that *should* knock the symbiote right off Henbane's body—which, in an enclosed space like the one just beyond the doorway, will create a vortex of inaudible sound that the alien being will be desperate to escape.

Cue the host hexahedron.

"Okay, just remember you have to aim it *right* at him and pull the trigger at precisely the right moment," Shuri says. "Wait for my cue. And remember: No matter what happens, do not scream. It will throw everything off."

"Right," the little Dora says with a nod. "Got it."

"Hopefully the blaster will be enough, and we won't need the sound cannon. That thing is *not* going to be fun in a space with those acoustics." She shakes her head but shoves the cylindrical tool into her coveralls pocket. "Ready?"

"ANY DAY NOW, LADIES!" Miles hollers as if on cue.

"Let's do this," the Karami replies.

As soon as they're back through the doorway and Shuri can now see the scene above their heads, she stops dead. And K'Marah crashes right into her.

"Ahh!" the little Dora shouts. "You almost made me drop the blaster thingy!"

But the princess doesn't react. Just stands, catching the cube tucked beneath her arm, with her gaze high and mouth agape. Because some three meters up, there are so many strings of webbing stretched across the cavern in multiple directions, they've created a veritable, though haphazard, spiderweb.

And above that? Across from each other on the dome-shaped ceiling—which is lower than Shuri expected—are two people-shaped spidery beings. Both with chests out and clinging to the stone walls by their fingertips and the soles of their feet. Venbane is easily recognizable, what with his "smile" of pointy-fanged death.

But the other guy . . . There's a mask over his entire head, but he's in a similar full bodysuit, also with a spider emblem at the center of the chest.

"*Miles?*" Shuri says.

"I *knew* something was up with that guy!" K'Marah says, stepping up beside the princess. "When he randomly vanished in the forest and then popped back up with his clothes all wonky . . . after he swung over our heads and stuck that big monkey's hands to his face—"

"Venbane no like Spider-Man!" the symbiote bellows. "Spider-Man hurt Venom! Venom Venbane only friend! Spider-Man bad!"

"That wasn't me, man! It was the other—"

But Miles doesn't get to finish.

Venbane leaps from his perch toward Miles, wicked sharp teeth bared and claws outstretched.

The princess's breath catches.

But at the last possible second, Miles fires off some webbing and swings himself across the space and out of harm's way. For the moment, at least.

"You all ready?" Miles calls down.

Shuri looks at K'Marah, and their eyes go wide.

"Ahh . . . almost!" the little Dora calls up into the air. "Not to be pushy, but if you could SPEED IT UP A BIT?"

"Yes! We are on it!" Shuri scurries to the opposite

end of the cavern and into position. "Okay!" she shouts as she opens the cube.

She gives K'Marah a thumbs-up, and the Dora raises the blaster, ready to shoot.

"We are ready!" Shuri shouts up to Miles.

"Okay, I'm going to slice through some of this web and—"

A thick cord of Venbane's webbing shoots in Miles's direction and manages to attach to his right shoulder.

"Gaaaah!" the Brooklyn boy yelps. And though Shuri can't see clearly from this far away, it looks like the stuff is eating through Miles's suit. "MAN, that *burns*!" he says.

K'Marah lets out a little shriek, but then covers her mouth. She and Shuri lock (Cat)eyes.

"Miles, are you okay?" Shuri hollers.

"Fine, fine, just . . . Maybe slowly dying, but I'll be cool. No worries!"

"Spider-Man talk too much!" Venbane snarls. The sound of his voice is even more gruesome in the echoey rock room.

"Gods!" K'Marah says. "How does he not *die* every time he speaks—?"

But she gets cut off when Miles yells as the symbiote yanks him from his post. The smaller spider-dude manages to shoot some of his own webbing in

Venbane's general direction—likely difficult to aim when you're being dragged through the air on a string like some dysfunctional yo-yo—and one of the shots hits the arm Venbane is using to pull Miles, while a second one hits the symbiote smack in his big white eye.

Venbane hollers and lifts his hand to his face, releasing the length of dense filament Miles is attached to. The rope of web retracts back into the symbiote's hand.

And thank Bast for the boy's quick reflexes: He rotates and aims another shot of his own stringy goop at the ceiling and manages to catch himself before making contact with the messy pseudo-spiderweb. "WHEW!" he says once he's back stuck to the upper cave wall. He hits Venbane with another sticky shot to the face. Then another. And another. The creature howls.

"*That* ought to hold his attention for a bit," Shuri says, watching the symbiote furiously shake his head and then try to remove some of the tacky stuff from his eyes.

Miles hits him again, this time gluing the symbiote's hand to his face.

"Spider-Man DIE!" Venbane bellows, trying to pull it away.

"Not today, pal!" Miles replies. Then he crawls down the curved rock a bit, spider-style (*so bizarre!*), and quickly looks around. "Ah-ha!" he says.

He dives off the wall toward the definite-death-trap web.

Shuri couldn't speak if she tried.

Luckily, his slim body slips through a hole with mere centimeters of circumference to spare, and he lands on his hands and springs off them, flipping to his feet.

"Wow" is all the princess can muster.

Miles runs over to her. "I'm gonna lure him down now, okay?" he says. "Just, whatever you do, don't step underneath that." He points at the snarled mess above them. "There's a good chance some of it will fall when he comes down, and you do *not* want to get tangled up in it. And definitely try to stay away from his webbing. Because of his mutant host, it's definitely poisonous." He looks at the giant hole in the shoulder of his suit. The wound beneath has begun to heal—Shuri can tell by the way its blackened edges are actively drawing inward—but it's definitely *not* something she would like to experience.

"Okay, here we go!" he says, backing to the center of the cave. "K'Marah, stay out from underneath the web, okay? And get ready to blow!"

"READY!" K'Marah says.

And right on time.

"Spider-Man *DIIIIIIE!*" Venbane leaps from the wall. And just as Miles predicted, the symbiote drops right through the webby jumble, knocking some of it to the floor.

Shuri hears K'Marah squeal and watches in horror as her best friend jumps backward.

And very much *out* of position.

As Venbane stands upright, Miles shoots a web at the ceiling and pulls himself up through the hole the symbiote just created.

Which Shuri presumes is her cue.

"SONIC *BOOM*, K'Marah!" she shouts in the Dora Karami's direction as she herself drops to a knee to flip up the lid of the host hexahedron and hold the box in place.

Nothing happens.

"K'MARAH!" Shuri bellows.

Which just draws the symbiote's attention. He looks right at Shuri, then left at K'Marah . . . then up, clearly searching for Miles.

But just as he bends his knees to leap, something extraordinary happens: His entire form begins to vibrate.

"YES!" Shuri shouts. "Hold steady, K'Marah!"

"I can't believe it's working!" the little Dora replies. "I mean, I can't hear a single thing!"

"I can't *hear* anything, but it's making my arms and legs all tingly," Miles says from above. "Is it doing that to you guys?"

But neither Shuri nor K'Marah responds. Both girls are watching the spectacle taking place between them, utterly rapt.

"Shuri?" Miles calls out. "K'Marah?"

And at some point he must climb down because Shuri hears a sudden "What the—? *Whoa!*" from somewhere behind her head.

An appropriate response. Because there in the center of some random mountain cavern in the thick of the Jabari-Lands, the princess of Wakanda, her Dora Karami best friend, and their American visitor (who is apparently a Super Hero) are witnessing the dramatic—and rather violent-looking—forced separation of an alien symbiote from its host.

As they watch on, Henbane's feet stay planted while the symbiote stretches in Shuri's direction, slowly curling off Henbane like peeling paint. "It's about to detach!" Miles says. "Get ready to catch, Prin—"

A gooey black blob comes flying at Shuri . . . And she is *not* ready. "Ahhhh!" she screams, holding up the box but flinching and shutting her eyes. It flies past her and hits the wall. Then immediately tries to make for the exit. "Uh-oh," she says as her error sinks in. (*What is going* on *with her today?*)

"SOUND CANNON, SHURI!"

"Oh! Right!" She pulls the thing out of her pocket, and K'Marah grabs it from her hand as she whizzes by.

"Get back into position!" the Karami commands.

So Shuri drops to a knee again, facing the other direction.

The symbiote is fast—*very* fast.

But not as fast as Shuri's best friend.

The little Dora leaps over the slithering lump and whips around, pushing the button to fire the cannon right at it. The screeching noise is even more awful with reverb added, and Shuri's ears are beginning to ring. She's not sure how long she'll be able to hold the box without her head exploding—

There's a *FWUMP* that knocks her onto her rear end, followed by a *click*.

The sound shuts off.

"YES!" K'Marah shouts, shoving her fist into the air.

Shuri looks down. There inside her cube is a writhing black mass. She gasps, looking up at her friend.

But K'Marah's face has changed.

"Oh no!" she says, her gaze fixed somewhere behind the princess. "Henny!"

Shuri looks over her shoulder, and K'Marah takes off at a run as the Narobian boy begins to fall forward.

She won't get to him in time, Shuri thinks. And yes, she's much closer, but she can't seem to get her muscles to move. Her ears are still ringing.

"HENNY, NO!" K'Marah shouts, lunging for him. But she's not close enough. He topples—

Something white and gummy shoots through the air and wraps around the mutant boy's waist. It keeps his face from hitting the ground. Miles lowers him gently, and retracts his webbing.

Shuri exhales. Henbane's not her *favorite* person, obviously, but she will definitely need to speak with him and gather some information.

"We take it you were successful?" comes a woman's voice from the entryway. Shuri turns back and shields her eyes from the bright light coming in. Nakia has ducked inside, and Umela is right behind her. "Where is Miles?"

"Ahh . . ." Her eyes go wide as Miles's discarded warmth suit flies into the air on a string of web.

"What was that?" Nakia and Umela look over their shoulders . . .

And Miles, back to himself, lands silently behind K'Marah. "Well, that sure got interesting!" he says.

The women whip back around. After taking him in, they look at each other . . . then they both shrug. "Welp, mission accomplished," Nakia says. "Let us depart for home."

MISSION LOG

I HAVE NEVER BEEN MORE EXHAUSTED IN MY ENTIRE LIFE.

It took us one hour and forty-seven minutes to find our way back to the Ice Fortress. We only learned the formal name for the home of the Jabari leader because we asked just about everyone we passed how to find it.

The first few people merely shook their heads when we tried to describe the place. Which is how we wound up so lost. Also rather unhelpful: Umela—the only person with even a vague knowledge of the terrain—stayed behind to attend to Henbane until help arrived . . . And that was wholly contingent on *us* figuring out where we needed to go.

The fifth person we asked—a boy of no more than seven—gave us the name: "Ah, you are seeking the Ice Fortress," he said excitedly, and every member of our group swelled with hope. But our collective bubble was swiftly burst: "I do not know the way there, but best of luck to you on your journey!" And he waved and scampered off.

Eventually, Miles took matters into his own web-slinging hands and decided he would swing around a bit to find us a good route. (He is Spider-Man! Who would've guessed??)

Nakia was wary, of course, not knowing what K'Marah and I do about the boy's . . . other skill set. But he was able to convince her through some strange combination of charm and insistence that his ability to navigate someplace scary-sounding called "Manhattan" prepared him for precisely this type of exploratory challenge.

While he was gone, we encountered an older woman whom I shall never forget. She was carrying a basket of fresh fish along a mountain path a few meters beneath where we were awaiting Miles's return, and when we called to her, she looked, saw me, and smiled.

"You are the princess," she declared. "You have done ample good, but there is still a ways to go." She pointed at me then. "Stay vigilant! And remember that even when your curiosity leads you to places you do not expect, there is always *something* to be gleaned! Look for the aberration!"

And then she walked off.

Not half a minute later, Miles returned to lead us back to the path we'd missed, and we reached the fortress in no time.

Someone was sent to retrieve and transport Henbane and Umela, and Nakia assured us we would receive an update on his health as soon as Umela arrived somewhere with Kimoyo service. And the journey back to the plain through the forest was uneventful, but the hexahedron seemed to add fifty kilograms to my backpack. Figuratively speaking, of course.

There was a piloted transport vessel

waiting near Umela's Asili cottage when we arrived—my beloved Msingi is nothing if not efficiently resourceful—and by the time we were airborne en route to the palace, everyone had fallen asleep except for the pilot and me.

It was a long and excruciating flight with all that time to think after such a strange mission.

Miles will depart tomorrow morning, and we agreed to discuss the *what to do* at breakfast. I have a hunch that he will want to take the symbiote back to America. I would assume that Fury expects it to travel—completely contained—back to the United States with Miles. Hence him sending Miles to our aid.

At any rate, there is still one question plaguing me: How did the symbiote get into Wakanda?

I am certain that until I have the answer, I will be restless.

Especially with the specimen in question currently sitting on a shelf in my closet.

17

HOLE

And restless she is.

In fact, for the bulk of at least two hours after retiring to her quarters, Shuri lies in bed on her back, staring up at her canopy. The sheer navy fabric is embroidered with phosphorescent thread so that when the lights are turned off, the princess can sleep beneath a cloth night sky, glowing constellations and all.

In truth, she rarely notices the thing; it's been there for years, hung during the astrophysics-obsessed phase she went through in early primary school. It was exciting at first, but now that she's older and has much more going on, most nights she tends to flop into bed on her stomach and drop right into slumber.

On *this* night, though, she can't stop staring at the thing. Because now, in addition to the question of how the symbiote got in, Shuri has a myriad of *other* thoughts and queries swirling.

It was decided that she would keep the contained specimen in her dressing chamber until morning. She told the others it was for lack of a better place to hide the thing from the queen mother without storing it off-site somewhere—her dressing chamber *does* have a rarely used sliding door that seals the space shut, and there are no vents or cracks or passageways out of there. Even if the symbiote were to somehow get free from the host hexahedron, it would be trapped inside the smallish space.

In truth, however, she didn't want the thing out of her reach.

Once the adrenaline wore off—and maybe the energizing tincture Umela used on her wounds as well—it occurred to Shuri that she had an *actual* extraterrestrial being sitting within a container that *she* created.

From there, the questions began to spill over the edges of her mind like the contents of a beaker on a too-hot Bunsen burner. What is the creature *made* of? What is its texture and/or consistency? How long can it survive without a host? Does it have a consciousness even when detached from a human? Could it bond with *any* carbon-based organism? Can it separate into smaller pieces? Would they be sentient?

Shuri's eyes are drawn—yet again—toward her dressing chamber. As she'd placed the cube up on the high shelf, the amorphous symbiote inside it had pushed itself up against the front transparent wall as if beckoning Shuri closer. The princess had placed her hand against the outside of the container, and the symbiote responded by morphing its form into the shape of her palm and spread fingers.

She was sorely tempted to open the cube right then and there.

What she wouldn't give to have just a few weeks with the writhing gelatinous mass. Learn more about it. See what it can do.

As strange as she feels about it, the princess is experiencing no small measure of guilt over not being able to give the symbiote what it was looking for. It was so convinced that Shuri had the little celestial rock; if only it had been right.

She sighs and her gaze is drawn back to the faux star–scattered canopy above her. So close to what's *out there* (because now it's literally *in here*). And yet so far away.

Shuri shuts her eyes and allows the fight to leech from her limbs. Perhaps some viable reason she should keep the being in Wakanda will occur to her by morning.

◇◇◇◇

It would seem that triple-teaming, sonic-blasting, and capturing an alien in a box has a similar affect on the princess's brain as the Kocha's phobia immersion therapy: She has another lucid dream.

At the start, she's inside her dressing chamber, looking for something, but not being entirely sure what—

Then it clicks: the nebular gem.

She checks every item of clothing with pockets, looks inside every bejeweled pair of shoes, pulls out the experimentation station and shakes the contents of each jar and vial (except for the two she knows *not* to shake), and goes through every cabinet and drawer.

It's not in there.

Her eyes are drawn to a transparent and vaguely shimmery cube on a shelf above her head. The lid is open, and the cube is empty.

This gives Shuri pause. While she can't seem to remember what belongs *inside* the cube (though the words *host hexahedron* floats through her mind . . . bizarre), a sinking feeling in her stomach tells her something's . . . off.

No time to think much about it: The word *gem* pops into her mind unbidden, and in an odd, gravelly voice.

I don't have it, she thinks but doesn't say.

The voice answers back, *You have. Must remember.*

She exits the dressing chamber.

After a quick look through the drawers in her bedside table and a peek into the cabinets within her personal bathroom (nothing), Shuri reaches for her Kimoyo card, and almost without her brain's permission, shuts off all the alarm sensors along a path through the palace, though she can't seem to puzzle out the destination . . .

Then things get *very* strange: She creeps out of her bedroom window and scales down the outer palace wall, using only her fingertips and toes. When she'd put on shoes, she doesn't know, but a quick glance down reveals her to be crawling, arachnid-style down the side of the palace, very much in her pajamas.

When she reaches the side entrance to the west wing on the ground floor, she puts her Kimoyo bracelet up to the digital lock-pad, and hears the bolt slide free.

She slips inside.

The next few moments are a blur. Literally. One moment she's hearing the heavy door click shut behind her, and the next, she's facing a blank wall in a hallway with no doors at all. And she's more than a little dizzy.

Princess body still metabolizing poison, the gravel voice says. *Heal tincture work, but Henbane poison strong. Give princess vertigo after high-speed motion.*

Huh? Shuri thinks.

New words, the voice continues. *Tincture: remedy made by dissolving medicine in alcohol. Metabolize: break down by natural chemical process within body of living thing. Vertigo: sensation of whirling and loss of balance. Princess head filled with many words. Too much for one head. Impractical.*

Then Shuri's hand lifts and reaches for the wall. Which is when she realizes she's standing outside the entrance to the vault of relics.

Panic rises in her throat just as it occurs to her that she didn't shut off the security cameras when she deaded the alarm system. She looks over her shoulder at the blinking red light near the ceiling—

No show face!

And her head whips back around of its own accord.

"You need to wake up now, Shuri!" she shouts into the air.

Not dream. Princess no yell.

"But I want to wake up now!"

Just want gem. Check vault, get gem.

"It's NOT in there!" Shuri attempts to lower her arm. Keep it from making contact with the smooth expanse of eggshell brown. *Who chose these paint colors?* she thinks as she struggles against her own limb. *Go DOWN, arm!*

It's to no avail. *No. Use Princess. Get gem. Henbane no help. Princess help. Princess have gem.*

Her hand surges forward, and the moment her palm makes contact, a hidden panel slides open to her right, revealing a touchscreen keypad.

"No, no, NO!" Shuri whispers aloud.

Princess no talk! the voice says. Then Shuri's fingers are swiftly ghosting over the numbers in the right order. There are fifteen—double the number of digits the average human can memorize, plus one more. When T'Challa taught her the sequence shortly after Baba's burial—at least three members of the royal family were required to know it, and there were only three left—Shuri had utilized an elaborate mnemonic to lock it into her head.

The pad turns green, and a retinal scanner slides out.

She squeezes her eyelids shut.

Princess OPEN eye, the voice says, and her right one pops wide.

After the successful scan, the panel of wall directly in front of the princess—and the visitor she appears to be hosting—slides free, revealing a hallway beyond that curves to the left.

I am NOT taking you in there! Shuri says to the voice, resisting forward motion. Her feet creep toward the threshold, very much *without* her permission, but she's able to keep them from crossing over. "No!" she says out loud again.

And then it hits her: *There is a fail-safe!* she thinks as loudly as she can. *A secondary security mechanism!*

Princess lie! the voice replies.

No! I mean it! The moment we step into this hall-way, the door will seal shut behind us, and the queen mother will be alerted! The only way back out will involve her opening the door from the outside!

For a moment, the princess's mind is eerily quiet (all things considered). The she hears: *Princess no lie. Princess tell truth. No want see shiny lady. Now plan B . . .*

Shuri's hand lifts again to shut the hidden door, then as soon as she blinks, she's on the move.

She's through the palace and at the exit to the staff quarters in what couldn't be more than a few seconds. Another blink, and she's leaving the palace grounds. Then she's at the edge of the Golden City. Then racing across the plain.

So fast, she fades in and out of consciousness. *Is that possible in a dream?*

The voice responds: *No Dream. Henbane poison bad. Princess sleep while blood fight poison.*

Wait . . . *What do you mean, slee—*

And then she's flying.

It's the forward momentum—and the drop of her stomach into her ankles—that coax her eyelids open . . . (Though she doesn't remember closing them?)

What Shuri sees, though, takes her breath away: She's soaring through the mountains—plunging down, then up, then forward, and again, down, up, forward. A perfect parabola with each swing. There's the Jabari fertile plateau with all its varieties of ice-dusted produce. And then the city, dark and silent as a tomb (and she would know from her time in the Necropolis). Thick, sticky black ropes—*no, strings of web!* she realizes—shoot from her wrist and attach themselves to high cliffs and mountain peaks that she swoops by.

It's nothing short of exhilarating.

Ah! Princess see now! Feel good! Not monster!

How did you learn to do this? Shuri asks what is now clearly the symbiote. *This might be the best dream I've ever had!* "Feel free to stay asleep now, self!" she says aloud into the wind.

Not dream. Learn spider tricks from friend Venom.

Wait, you KNOW Venom? She swoops into the next arc.

Sent to Venom good teacher. Good friend. Venom Klyntar, too.

Ah, Shuri thinks. Then, *Wheeeee! I never want this to end . . .*

But a few swings later, her feet are landing on a tiny ledge in the face of a cliff wall. And then she's crawling up, up, up on her fingertips and toes. (*I'm a SPIDER!* she thinks.)

When Shuri reaches the top and looks around, she almost can't believe what she's seeing: her beloved nation stretched out before her. There's Birnin S'Yan, Wakanda's southernmost city, founded by Shuri and T'Challa's uncle. There's Birnin Zana, the Golden City and Wakandan capital, where Shuri's home lies, and there's the Necropolis just outside it. There's the Sacred Mound, source of all Vibranium. The baobab plain. Birnin Azzaria, Birnin Bashenga, Birnin Djata, Birnin T'Chaka.

And there are the mountains she's standing in. The Jabari village and M'Baku's Ice Fortress.

This is *her* kingdom full of *her* people. And looking out over all of it, Shuri knows beyond a shadow of a doubt that it is *her* job to both protect what is here *and* figure out a way to do good in the wider world with it—

No gem. Now time.

The princess has no idea what the symbiote means by that, but there's a faint *buzz* overhead. And though Shuri wouldn't say she can "hear" it, the sound causes a distinct tingle in her legs. So she looks up.

There above her is an egg-shaped hole in the sky.

Before she can think much about it, however, an ear-shattering screech fills the air. And though the princess can feel it coming from her own mouth, she can't seem to stop it.

Then everything goes black.

18
INVASION

Shuri's alarm blares, and she bolts upright in her bed as if pulled by a string. (Or . . . *web*, perhaps?) Her eyes shift around the room. The princess knows she had a *very* strange dream and that it involved the sensation of flying and falling over and over. The details are gone, but it must have been a wild one: She's intensely fatigued, as though she hasn't slept a wink.

She slowly climbs out of bed, shocked at just how much her body aches . . . though she guesses it makes sense considering the trek through the mountains yesterday? An attempted stretch alerts her to soreness in her shoulders and back that's more pronounced than she would've expected considering the hike involved mostly her leg muscles . . . but maybe it's from carrying the backpack?

She eyes her bedside tables. Even goes so far as to open the drawers. Everything is precisely where she left it.

Same thing with her reading nook and bookshelves.

Yet still: Despite how silly it makes her feel, the princess can't shake the sense that there was another presence here in her room.

She blinks and has a flash of the host hexahedron . . . but it's empty.

Quick as she can muster, Shuri stumbles over to the shut door of her dressing chamber. (*Wow*, does her body ache!) She shoves it open and almost trips over her own feet to get inside, then rushes over to check the high shelf near the experimentation station—

The symbiote is writhing around inside the clear cube, just as she left it. (But it appears as though the creature is trying to find a way out.)

Shuri exhales.

She considers Kimoyo calling K'Marah, then realizes she has no idea what time it is. Has she missed breakfast with Miles? Shuri looks back at the symbiote. They're supposed to discuss what to *do* with it . . .

And then something comes over Shuri. A resolve. She will keep the symbiote here in Wakanda and build a larger polycarbonate receptacle so that she can study it.

She takes a step closer, drawn toward the boxed creature as if by magnetism. Or maybe something even stronger. Like . . . kinship.

The princess reaches for the container, and as soon as she makes contact, she experiences a series of disjointed flashes: the empty box (again); the wide-open entrance to the vault of relics; the central plain underfoot; the lush Jabari farmlands; mountains flying by (or was *she* flying by *them*?); a sweeping view of most of her nation; a hole in the sky—

She gasps and pulls her hands back. The black mass presses itself against the front of the box. It forms itself into the shape of a hand.

Shuri shakes her head and slowly steps backward.

Another flash. This one of her same hands on that same transparent box. Pulling it down from the shelf. Pressing the tiny release button on the side and lifting the lid.

"No," she whispers, continuing to back away. "No, no, no . . ."

The blob had pulled back into a corner at first, but then slowly crept forward and up the side. Down over her hand—

There's a *bang bang bang* on her door, and the princess startles so intensely, she trips over her own feet, landing on her bottom with an *OOMPH*.

"Shuri!" a voice calls into the room. "Shuri, you must come! We have to—"

A siren sounds in the distance.

Then another one, closer by.

Then a third.

Then the palace alarm.

"Shuri, where *are* you?"

Fast footsteps cross the marble floor of the princess's bedroom. Then a person appears in the closet doorway.

Nakia.

Her beloved Msingi. Should she tell the Dora of the things she's seen (inside her mind, at least)?

"Your Majesty, why are you sitting on the floor? You must come immediately. Where are your clothes?" Nakia shuffles around the dressing chamber in search of something for Shuri to wear. "All these things are so *impractical*," she says.

It makes Shuri smile.

"Ah-ha!" Nakia exclaims. "Put this on." Something

is laid out on the floor at Shuri's side. "In five minutes, I will return to retrieve you. Be sure to grab every sound-based weapon in your possession."

That gets Shuri's attention. She sits up on her elbows. "Huh?"

"Can you not hear the alarms, Shuri? We are in the midst of a national emergency! *Please* peel yourself from the floor and get dressed! You are desperately needed!"

"Needed for *what*?"

Nakia huffs and comes to kneel beside the princess. She points to the cube containing the symbiote. "That thing? The one you trapped? There are more of them."

Shuri suddenly remembers a frightful screech. And the hole in the sky.

"They have taken possession of our countrymen, Your Highness. And you, it seems, are the only person left who knows how to get rid of them."

◇◇◇◇◇

By the time Nakia reappears, Shuri is not only dressed in what her Msingi chose for her (and admittedly impressed with the Dora's selection), she's got her backpack on and is ready to move.

Well, for the most part: Her body still aches as though she participated in some sort of gladiator-style obstacle course competition like the ones she's seen

T'Challa watching. But no matter: She will give this—whatever it is—all she's got.

And oddly enough, the princess thinks she has an idea.

"I will need to visit my laboratory," she tells Nakia as they rush out of the palace. "Is there a transport vessel we can take?"

"Right there on the left, Your Majesty. It's there for you."

"And K'Marah and Miles?"

"Miles, unfortunately, departed hours ago. Which means *you* are our sole source of black-blobby-alien expertise. K'Marah went with Ayo and General Okoye to provide reinforcements just outside Birnin Bashenga. They could be anywhere."

Miles is already gone?

"The good news is that your dear brother returned around the same time Miles was departing. And though I haven't seen for myself, word is that one of those American Super Hero individuals came with him."

Shuri has many questions, but they're all jockeying for position at the front of her mind, so she can't seem to single one out.

What she manages: "And Mother? Where is she?"

"She is inside the central security room at the

palace, helping with the deployment of guards to the areas where they are most needed. Between the two of us, the queen might be headed into a new career as a military tactician."

This makes Shuri smile.

Once they're strapped in and leaving the ground, Nakia begins to fill the princess in on what's been happening.

"Just before dawn, we received reports of abnormal activity in the foothills of the mountains just north of Birnin Djata. A cattle farmer ran into the city complaining of 'a pair of strange and terrifying creatures feasting on his cows,'" she says. "This matched complaints from early last week before we knew that the 'person' wreaking havoc in Birnin Zana and across the plain was your creature—"

"Symbiote." Shuri shifts uncomfortably in her seat and eyes her backpack on the floor at her feet.

"Hmm?"

"The creature is an alien symbiote." *And he can likely hear you calling him a "creature,"* Shuri doesn't say.

"Ah. Yes, well, *now* we seem to be in the thick of a full-blown . . . symbiotic alien invasion," Nakia continues. "After that initial call, more came in. Reports of four crawling up the side of the central clock tower in Birnan T'Chaka; an unknown quantity ripping through the marketplace in Birnan Bashenga; a pair ravaging a grove of mango trees in the fertile plateau; there are even reports of some invading the lakes and devouring the fish. It's like nothing we've ever seen before."

Shuri stares down at her bag and remembers a hole in the sky. The keening screech that issued from her throat but very distinctly wasn't hers.

The hole wasn't in the *actual* sky . . . it was in the dome. *That's* how the symbiote got in after leaving Narobia.

And she can only presume it's how the others got in, as well.

"And they've all taken hosts?" Shuri asks more to the contained black blob hidden in her backpack than to Nakia.

But Nakia responds: "It would appear so," she says. "*Who* those hosts are is a mystery, but the 'symbiotes,' as you put it, are definitely moving in bipedal humanoid forms."

"Wow, Nakia," Shuri says. "You are beginning to sound like me."

"I have a master's degree in biology, dear." The Dora winks.

As they soar southwest in the direction of the Sacred

Mound, the princess can see some of the havoc below. A group of no fewer than thirty symbiote-covered hosts—who Shuri presumes are all Wakandan—is charging across the plain in the direction of Birnin Azzaria, a small city just south of the Sacred Mound. Wakanda's Learned City. It contains the largest population of academics and philosophers, Scholar M'Walimu included. Maybe she should put in a Kimoyo call to the fossil of a man and ask him to chastise the symbiotes back to their home planet. "Perhaps *they're* going to learn a thing or two," Shuri says.

Soon, the princess and her Msingi are touching down by the entrance to the cave that houses Shuri's lab. "You can go," the princess says to their pilot. "I will transport us from here."

The man looks at Nakia for confirmation.

"Well?" the Dora says, clearly peeved. "Are you going to heed the princess's directive, or be insubordinate?"

That sure straightens him up. Literally: He sits stock upright in his seat. "Yes, Your Highness." He nods reverently at Shuri. "My sincerest apologies."

"Don't let it happen again," Nakia says. "As you were, Princess."

Shuri isn't sure how to respond, so she doesn't initially. *Is this what it feels like to be treated as something other than a small child?* she thinks as she and Nakia traverse the cave corridor to her laboratory entrance. Once they're inside and the door has closed behind them, sealing them in, Nakia turns to Shuri. "So what can I do to help?" she asks.

Shuri has never felt so . . . warm inside. It almost brings tears to her eyes, this grown-up not questioning her capabilities. "Ahh . . . I'm not *exactly* sure yet, but once I figure it out, I will let you know."

"Understood."

Shuri heads to the left lab station and goes directly to the panel in the wall that leads to her weapons arsenal. Not even K'Marah knows it's here.

"Ahh, Nakia?" she says, realizing she actually does need help. "I *could* use your assistance with something . . . but I also need you to not freak out? Or like . . . tell my mother of what you're about to see."

"I am your Msingi," the Dora says, making her way to the princess. "The designation exists for good reason."

After an intensive deep breath, Shuri presses the button that reveals the palm scanner and then places her hand against it. A section of wall slides free, revealing a small chamber lined on three sides with weapons of various shapes and sizes. There are different types of gauntlets that fit on the hands like a glove, and objects that are shaped like firearms but utilize mechanisms such as high-frequency sound waves and small electromagnetic pulses instead of projectiles like bullets. (So primitive.) There's even a row of what looks like panther stuffed toys that release different chemical compounds capable of incapacitating an opponent long enough to run away.

"Uhhh . . . wow," Nakia says, peeking inside. "Quite the setup you have here."

Shuri smiles. "Most of these are prototypes, but there's an entire section devoted to the use of sound waves. Here." She hands Nakia a larger version of the sonic blaster they used to blow the symbiote off Henbane's body. "I have to admit: This haven't been tested. So let us pray to Bast that they will actually be useful."

After grabbing a few other objects—a pair of gauntlets that have both sonic *and* electromagnetic capabilities, a Frisbee-shaped device that emits a high-pitched howl when thrown, and one of the stuffed panthers that releases a noxious laughing gas—the princess and her Msingi walk through the laboratory kitchen to the hangar where Shuri keeps her personal transport vessel, the *Predator*.

"Oh my," Nakia says, walking around the panther-shaped craft. "I've heard stories of this thing, but to see it with my own eyes . . . the general did *not* do it justice with her lackluster description."

Shuri smiles at the memory of General Okoye accompanying her to a salt flat wasteland in Ethiopia to rescue a group of kidnapped girl geniuses, K'Marah included. These Dora Milaje ladies aren't so bad after all.

They board the *Predator* and head out.

"Soooo . . . where should we start?" Shuri says.

"Excellent question," Nakia replies. "I think maybe we need to figure out what's happening where."

"Valid." There's a part of Shuri that is anxious to plunge into the fray . . . but what exactly could she do? Alien symbiotes running amok doing who-knows-what who-knows-where isn't exactly a thing the princess—or anyone in Wakanda, for that matter—has ever encountered before.

"All right," she says. "I guess we can begin with some terrain scans."

It takes fewer than seven minutes for Shuri and Nakia to discover that the situation on the ground is far worse than either could've ever imagined. The symbiotes are *everywhere*.

"Initial count has us at one hundred and fifty-two of the organisms," the princess says, reading the results aloud. "Eighty-nine of them took hosts who were wearing Kimoyo bracelets, so I could potentially utilize the Kimoyo-capture mechanism to gather *that* group, but . . . I don't know what we would do with them. Any host who is bonded with a symbiote will be possessed of superhuman strength, speed, and agility," Shuri continues. "So, barring some sort of confined area we could drop them into—and I certainly can't think of one—the moment we let them go, they'll likely run off. That's not to mention the sixty-three that we have no means of capturing. Plus, who-knows-how-many the scan might've missed."

"This . . . isn't good," Nakia says.

"That certainly bears repeating . . ." Shuri worries her bottom lip between her teeth. She has an idea—has *had* an idea since experiencing what she can only assume was some sort of flashback when she touched the cube earlier. But she knows how outlandish it's going to sound to her Msingi. Yes, Nakia has been fantastic thus far and has trusted Shuri's judgment on just about everything. But *this* has the potential to break all that.

She takes a deep breath and forges ahead anyway. "Okay, so . . . I *think* I may know what to do?"

Nakia looks at her expectantly, and Shuri gulps. "Be forewarned," she says, "this is likely to sound absolutely absurd . . . But I can't see any other way—"

"Spit it out, Your Majesty," the Dora says. "Lest you forget, I grew up running alongside your brother. There are some *stories* I could tell. Trust me."

Shuri eyes the small compartment where her backpack is stored. "Okay, well . . ." *UGH!* "Do you remember when K'Marah and I were speaking with Venbane behind that museum in Birnin Bashenga?'

"How could I forget?" Nakia replies with a shudder. "I was so terrified that the thing was going to eat you both, I could barely keep myself from launching my spear in his direction while you had him distracted!"

Shuri almost laughs. Almost.

"Well, he said something that I think might be related to our current predicament."

Nakia cocks her head. "Really?"

"Mm-hmm. I didn't think anything of it at the time, but . . ." Shuri sighs again, bothered that she didn't think to take the threat seriously when he said it. "When he was talking about the gem thing he came here to find, he said that . . . Well, he said that if I didn't give it to him, he would call his 'friends.'"

The Dora's eyes widen. "And you think that's what happened?"

"I think . . ." Shuri says, unable to hold Nakia's

gaze, "that I might've been there when said 'call' went out."

From there, Shuri tells her Msingi about the "lucid dream" she had that likely wasn't a dream at all. The parts she can remember at least . . . which include the hole in the dome and that terrible sound that ripped through the air from Shuri's open mouth.

"So you're saying *you* invited all these . . . beings here?"

"I mean, not exactly *me*. The symbiote was using my body."

"Uh-huh," Nakia says, crossing her arms. "And precisely how did the symbiote *get* to your body, Princess?"

"That's . . ." *Oh boy.* Probably shouldn't mention that, if the flashback she had earlier is accurate, she likely waltzed right into her dressing chamber and opened the container while half-asleep. ". . . neither here nor there, Nakia. The point is, I have an idea of what to do to get all the symbiotes to gather in one place."

Shuri watches suspicion creep onto her Msingi's face. This is going more poorly than she anticipated.

"Before you share this clearly harebrained idea, based on the way you are *hedging*, do tell me: Precisely what will we *do* with these symbiotes once you've accomplished your gathering mission?"

"Well . . . my hope is that I'll be able to talk them into leaving. But I'll . . . need some assistance."

Nakia shuts her eyes and shakes her head. "Do I even want to know what you are going to say next?"

"Probably not, but I have to say it anyway, don't I?"

"Yes," Nakia says. "Yes, you do. Spit it out."

Shuri stares in the direction of her stowed backpack. "I think I have to achieve symbiosis."

19

SYMBIOSIS

Nakia . . . doesn't get it. "You need to *what*?"

"Oh, come on, biology master!" Shuri says, looping around the plain again for another scan. "You know what symbiosis is!"

"Of course, I know what symbiosis *is*, but . . ."

The map screen lights up with four concentrated clusters of oddly shaped blobs and a few random scattered dots. Shuri launches a three-dimensional rendering into the air.

"Are you suggesting what I *think* you are suggesting?" Nakia continues, working her way to the nitty-gritty. "You want to . . . *bond*? With one of those things?"

"Not just *any* one. The one I think I already bonded with. I have him . . ." Shuri swallows and looks sheepishly at the Dora. "In my backpack?"

"You *what*??" Nakia's head whips around, completely ignoring the floating map and highlighted masses moving about on it. "Here, Shuri? You have an alien *here*? As in on this vessel with *us*?"

"Ahh . . . yes," the princess replies. "I grabbed it from my closet just in case—"

"Just in case *what*, Your Majesty?"

"In case we needed it, Nakia! Look for yourself!" Shuri gestures to the map. "The beings are everywhere! T'Challa and our foot soldiers and you lovely Dora Milaje are all excellent in combat, but you must admit that this is a different type of threat. The symbiotes are not only faster than even T'Challa, they have sharper claws and mouths full of razor-sharp fangs! The one *we've* been dealing with can *climb walls* and *hang from ceilings* and shoot this *webby* stuff that gives him the ability to basically *fly* from place to place—"

"Okay, okay, I see your point." Nakia raises her hands.

"I wouldn't suggest it if I didn't think it potentially benefic—"

But Shuri stops as her eyes lock onto the compartment where her book bag is stored. "Wait one minute," she says, slowly approaching the space.

"Ahh . . . Princess?"

But Shuri ignores her Msingi. And when she pulls open the slender door, it's not the backpack she reaches for. There's a shelf above where the bag is hanging, and on that shelf, there is a small box. "How could I have forgotten?" Shuri says below her breath as she pulls it down.

"Forgotten what, Your Highness?"

Shuri is so focused on the box, Nakia's voice startles her, and she almost drops it. "Eeks!" she shouts.

"My apologies," Nakia says. "But, ahh . . . what's in the box?"

Shuri doesn't respond, just sets it down and takes a deep breath, hoping her sudden hunch is a good one.

"Princess?" Nakia presses.

"Do you remember that invasion attempt by Zanda of Narobia a while back?"

Nakia's face darkens. "How could I forget? That senseless woman has had a *thing* for your brother for years."

Shuri swallows her chuckle. "Well, I didn't think about it until just now, but before Queen Ororo left to return to Kenya, she handed me this box. 'To the winner go the spoils' is what she said. And she winked."

"Okay . . ."

"I only gave it a brief glance then because there was so much transpiring. I shoved it into the closet over there and forgot all about it until just now . . ." Shuri flips the lid open, and whatever words she would've said next dry up and disintegrate on her tongue.

"Wow, that thing is hideous," Nakia says, peeking over Shuri's shoulder at the overwrought golden cuff covered in various gemstones. Shuri recognizes a piece of tanzanite, a very large diamond, and a small hunk of Wakandan Vibranium (*where had she acquired* that?) among a smattering of other rare and precious gems.

It's not lost on the princess that the evil giantess Zanda truly *is* some sort of collector—the amount of wealth she could've acquired by selling off just a few of these *known* sparkly rocks is astonishing. But the one Shuri *really* cares about—

"You see that pale pink stone at the center?"

"It would be so much prettier if it weren't attached to that ghastly thing. I'm guessing it belonged to Zanda? Only *she* would ever consent to wear something that tacky."

There's no holding back the snort this time. And

Shuri is thankful; it breaks the tension she's feeling. She really *can* fix this.

She thinks . . .

"I'm pretty sure that's"—Shuri lowers her voice in case the symbiote is listening (this makes her feel more than a little ridiculous, but oh well)—"the nebular gem."

"The what?"

"Shhhhhh!" Shuri glances at the closet. "This is what the original symbiote intruder was looking for. I've apparently had it the whole time and didn't realize."

"Okay . . ."

"I think I can use it to get them all to leave . . ."

"It sounds like there is a 'but' coming?"

"Well," Shuri says, resolving to at least give her plan a try. She goes back to the closet and retrieves the cube this time. Nakia shrieks and stumbles over the copilot's chair, and it takes everything in the princess not to laugh. "As I mentioned before," she continues, "I think that in order to pull it off, we are going to need *his* assistance."

◇◇◇◇◇

They bring the *Predator* down just above the baobab plain—the only area the symbiotes have stayed away from. (Odd, but Shuri tries not to think too much of it.)

"Will you keep watch?" the princess asks her Msingi. "I need to, umm . . . get dressed."

Nakia looks more wary than Shuri's ever witnessed, but she complies. And the moment she's off the vessel, Shuri pops opens the host hexahedron and sticks her hand inside. "All right," she says to the wriggling black form. "Let's get on with it."

It slowly creeps up her hand and then wraps around her arm before spreading itself over the rest of her body. It feels like a bucket of cool, viscous liquid overtaking her bit by bit until it envelops the top of her head, fingertips, and toes simultaneously. The moment the bonding is complete, the symbiote starts yakking in Shuri's head.

Princess have gem. You find. I take.

And the princess can feel her body turning toward where she stashed the box with Zanda's jillion-U.S.-dollar cuff.

WAIT! And she successfully resists the movement. Guess there's something to be said about being *awake* while bonded.

Gem from Klyntar. I take. Can see in mind.

STOP poking around in there, Shuri replies. *It is a flagrant invasion of privacy!*

No can resist. Much chaos in Princess brain. Like flea market. "How rude!" Shuri says aloud. Which she only knows because Nakia comes running.

And stops dead when she actually *sees* Shuri. "Uhhh . . . Princess?"

Shuri waves but doesn't speak. She knows what that voice sounds like and would rather not shred her *own* eardrums and her Msingi's at the same time.

Nakia nods but doesn't come any closer. "Sooooo . . . not to be, ahhh . . . *discourteous*. But as your *pal* is a symbiote, is it possible for him to take on *your* form instead of the other way around?"

Huh . . . I hadn't even thought of that, Shuri thinks. *Can we do that?* she asks the symbiote.

"Ah, much better!" Nakia says.

Shuri turns to look at her faint reflection in one of the *Predator*'s windows. She looks precisely like herself. "Huh," she says.

"Now we can walk places together without it looking like I am fraternizing with the enemy."

Not en—!

"He's not our enemy!" Shuri says aloud, finishing the symbiote's thought *and* trying to keep him from getting angry. It might be the strangest *mental* thing she's ever experienced. "In fact, he doesn't actually want to be here. He only came to Wakanda because he was looking for the nebular gem so he could get back home."

(Okay, she lied before. Strangest mental thing ever is seeing inside the mind and intentions of an alien symbiote and being able to communicate with them plainly.)

"So, what about the horde that arrived before dawn? You said *it* called them here, yes? Forgive my skepticism, but that sounds more like an attempt to make *this* home."

Shuri (*Or are we "Shurom" now? Vuri?*) shakes her head. "It only called them because I couldn't find the gem," she says. "It was . . . lonely and tired of feeling out of place." The light bulb pops on. "Just like Henbane."

"Okay," Nakia presses. "So if it was able to call its . . . cohorts, and they were able to just show up at will, why can't it return utilizing the same mechanism by which they arrived? Did they not come from the same planet?"

An excellent question, and one Shuri admittedly hadn't considered (which definitely feels a bit out of character for the princess, but it *has* been a peculiar week).

The answer hops to the tip of her tongue as if it's coming from her own mind: "It was exiled. For not wanting to . . . do bad things. So it can't teleport back and forth from there like they can."

"They answered the call of an *exiled* member of their kind?"

"They apparently like adventure." Shuri shrugs. "Earth seemed very 'shiny object.'"

"So what he's—"

"She now," Shuri says, surprising even herself.

"Excuse me?"

Shuri clears her throat. "We are *she*. Not *he*."

"Okay . . ." Nakia says. "My apologies. Might I continue?"

"Uhhh . . . yes. Sorry. Please do."

"So what you're saying is that the others are able to blink themselves back to their home planet the same way they arrived here?"

"Yes."

"And your . . . specimen *cannot* do that, but with this gem you mentioned, it would be possible for said specimen to *poof* him—I mean *her*self—out of here as well?"

"Yes."

"And she's *willing* to help us? And then leave?"

This is a question Shuri hadn't considered. So she asks, *Ahh . . . friend?*

Princess is friend now? The . . . sincerity with which he (she?) asks surprises Shuri. Also surprising is the burst of warmth in her chest. The symbiote really isn't so bad.

Yes, Shuri replies. *I am your friend. If I agree to give you the gem, will you help us gather the ... relatives you summoned and persuade them to return home?*

For a moment, there is silence inside Shuri's mind. Then: *Yes. Will help friend princess. Then take gem.*

Shuri smiles. "She has agreed to help."

"So they would be out of Wakanda completely? Never to return?"

"Well, the *never-to-return* part cannot be guaranteed, but yes, they will certainly be out of Wakanda."

Nakia nods resolutely. "All right," she says. "Understood. Now let's go and save our nation."

20
CAPTURE

Shuri—who currently looks like herself—sighs as she and Nakia (and her current symbiotic other half) make their way down onto the baobab plain to meet the others. "This is by far the most harebrained plan I have ever come up with," she says, seeing T'Challa, Okoye, Ayo, and K'Marah exit a hoverjet close to the spot where Shuri called them all to gather.

Also with them: Spider-Man. She smiles. "Sneaky, sneaky, Mr. Morales."

"Let's just hope your *plan* works," Nakia says.

K'Marah waves and breaks into a sprint, and Shuri

runs over the plan in her head one last time. When they're all together, she should be able to share it confidently . . . or at least without getting tongue-tied.

And the princess is *glad* she's currently bonded to the symbiote: Her Dora Karami best friend leaps and throws her arms *and* legs around Shuri, and thanks to the added strength in her muscles from her alien friend, Shuri is able to stay on her feet. "Oh my gods, I was so *worried*," K'Marah says.

"Worried about what, K'Marah?"

The shorter girl unwraps herself from the princess and drops back down to the ground. "Have you been doing push-ups or something?" she asks, giving Shuri a once-over. "I don't remember you being that strong . . ."

Nakia snorts. "You have no idea, Karami."

"What were you worried about?" Shuri says to K'Marah, trying to bring everyone back to center.

"I dunno, Shuri . . . maybe about that *thing* getting out of the box and trying to eat you? Have you *seen* the havoc these creatures are wreaking on this land that *you* are first in line to rule?"

Not THING! Siblings not CREATURES!

I know, I know. Calm down, Shuri replies to the symbiote.

"He's—"

SHE! The symbiote bellows in Shuri's head.

She takes a deep breath. "*She* isn't a 'thing,' K'Marah. She's a sentient being from another planet who just wants to go home."

"Wait, what do you mean *she*—"

"Yoooo!" Miles—or Shuri guesses she should say *Spider-Man* since he is in full costume—jogs over and puts his hands on his knees, panting. "These symbiotes have given your boy a *workout* today, man. Whew!"

"Ahhh . . . and who might *you* be?" Nakia asks the black-suited boy. Now that they're in the light—and she's not viewing him in monotone through night-vision glasses—Shuri can see that his suit is accented with red.

"Oh. Uhhh—"

"This is Spider-Man, Nakia. He is a great American Super Hero!"

It takes everything in the princess not to laugh. She shoves her hand out. "Lovely to meet you, Mr. Spider-Man, sir! Thank you for gracing us with your special skills!"

Miles clears his throat. "You're, uhhh . . . welcome. Your Majes-ness! I mean, Your Highnesty! I mean—"

"Shuri," T'Challa says with a nod of his head, cutting Miles off. He's also in costume but has his face mask removed. "Nakia."

"My king," Nakia returns, tippin' her head as well.

It takes everything in Shuri not to giggle over the grin tugging at the corner of Nakia's mouth and the very evident twinkle in her brother's eye.

Not sure we like Panther man, the symbiote says (and Shuri has to clench her teeth to keep the words from coming out of her mouth). *Panther man give bad vibe. Panther man angry.*

Hey, that's my brother, Shuri replies. *And cut him some slack.* Your brethren *are causing quite the uproar in this country that "Panther man" rules.*

"Lovely to see you, General," Shuri says aloud to Okoye before the symbiote can respond. Talking back to a voice inside her head while trying to interact with actual *people* is getting disorienting. "And you as well, Ayo."

"Your Highness. Nakia," the Dora Milaje women say in turn.

"All right!" T'Challa claps and clasps his hands together. "Now that we've gotten the formalities out of the way, how are we to solve this . . . problem?" he asks, jumping right to the point. (So typical.)

"Well, Shuri has a plan," Nakia says.

Shuri's symbiote partner laughs in her mind. It is not a pleasant pseudo-sound. *Hahahahaha warrior woman throw princess under bus!*

Shuri doesn't respond to her. "Yes," she says to the group instead. "I do. Ahh . . ."

And there's the tied tongue.

"Are you quite all right, Your Highness?" Okoye asks.

Princess tell them.

Shuri takes a deep breath and then launches in. "Okay," she says. "In a nutshell, as our recently departed friend *Miles* would say, we need to lure all the bonded symbiotes here to the baobab plain."

"And how do you propose we *do* that, Sister?"

"She will get there, T'Challa," Nakia says. (And Shuri's never been more grateful.) "Go on, Your Highness."

Shuri nods. "Once they are all here, I will summon the *Predator* to come hover above us all, and then I will cast a miniature dome over the plain utilizing the vessel's Kimoyo-capture mechanism. It will be inescapable, which hopefully will mean that we can get the symbiotes to separate from all the hosts and to volunteer to teleport back to their home planet peacefully."

"Okay," T'Challa says. "And if they won't?"

"Well, if they won't, we'll have to hit them with a magnified sonic blast that will flow from the dome itself. The frequency will be just above twenty-seven kilohertz, so we won't hear a thing, you included, Brother. But as K'Marah and I witnessed, the symbiotes will be blown right off their hosts. After which, I will vacuum them up into the airtight, sound-absorbent undercarriage of the *Predator*. And it will be made known to them that the only way they can escape is by leaving Wakanda and returning home."

T'Challa looks impressed.

"Not to be the pessimist party pooper—because that truly is a fantastic plan, best friend," K'Marah says then. "But I must return to your big brother's question: How, precisely, are we going to get them *here*?"

"Well . . ." Shuri peeks over her shoulder at Nakia—who (unhelpfully) gives her a look that says: *You're on your own here, Princess.*

"Well what, baby sis?" from T'Challa.

The princess turns back to face the others, then exhales, squares her shoulders, and lifts her chin. "I'm going to call them."

"Call them?" from Okoye this time.

"Yes. I will dispense weapons, and you all will hide over there behind the trunk of the baobab. Once the dome deploys, you will come out in case there's . . . a fight. They won't be able to just run away like they've been doing when you try to wrangle them."

"How could you possibly know that's what they've been doing, Shuri?" T'Challa asks.

"Uhh . . . Call it intuition," the princess replies, not quite ready to reveal that she's . . . not completely *only* herself and is getting *insider* info—literally.

Though said revelation is certainly about to happen.

"Let's get to it," she says, lowering her backpack and passing the gauntlets to Ayo, the sonic blaster to Nakia, the Frisbee to Spider-Man, and the poison-filled stuffed panther to K'Marah—who thankfully needs no explanation: The creation was her idea. "All of you, over there." She points to the trunk of the tree. It's as wide as a small house. "You'll know when to come out."

For a moment, everyone just stares at Shuri as though she's speaking a language they don't understand.

"I hope you know what you're doing, Princess," Nakia says in Shuri's ear in passing. Then louder to everyone: "All right, you heard her. Let's not dillydally. We have a small alien horde to get rid of."

They all turn to head to the tree. Shuri hears T'Challa say, "I . . . I don't understand what is happening."

"You'll be fine, Cha-Cha," Nakia replies, patting him on the back. "She's *your* little sister, after all, and you have been a spectacular role model, wouldn't you say?" The Dora peeks over her shoulder at Shuri and winks.

Which the princess takes as her cue.

"Okay, friend," she says aloud to her symbiote (and once she hears herself, feels quite odd about it). "Let's do this."

Friends work together, the symbiote replies. Now that she's conscious of being bonded, Shuri can sense a number of things she and the alien have in common: a longing to belong; a desire to be a part of something *bigger* than themselves; a want for the safety and comfort of *home*; a need for connection and friendship . . .

Oddly enough, the more Shuri allows herself to experience the alien symbiote's emotions, the more *human* and understood *she* feels.

That's right: Friends work together, she replies.

Before we make call, must warn: the others more . . . rough around edges. Not so nice.

"And yet you called them here anyway," Shuri says aloud, shaking her head.

You no give gem. Miss home, so bring home here.

"Yeah, yeah, yeah." She looks back to make sure she can't see any of the others—and that they can't see her—then closes her eyes and takes one final inhale of Wakandan air as herself (for now at least). *Go ahead and transform,* she says in her head this time. *Let's get this party started.*

Though Shuri doesn't *feel* any sort of transformation, when she lifts her hands to look at them, they're coated shimmery black with wicked sharp claws she can extend and contract at will. And yet she's still wearing her Kimoyo bracelet. "This is by far the *least* believable experience I've ever had."

Princess get ready. We call now. Princess no faint this time.

Shuri steadies herself and opens her mouth.

◈◈◈◈

The next thing Shuri knows, the symbiote is speaking in her mind again. *Princess fainted. Weak. Wake up now.*

Oh, shut up. She shakes her head, and once her vision clears, her instinct is to scream (though, of course, she doesn't; certainly can't blow her cover *now*). She has no idea how long it's been, but she's standing in the thick of at least a hundred symbiotic beings, all with claws out and teeth bared.

And all looking at her. There are yet more making their way down onto the plain.

As clandestinely as she can, Shuri runs a fingertip over one bead of her bracelet—to put the *Predator* in Invisi-mode—and then taps the one beside it to summon the vessel overhead. She just needs the alien-covered hosts to come in a *liiiiiittle* closer.

Are they all here? she asks the symbiote.

Three more, he replies. *Eight seconds.*

Excellent.

Almost on cue, the final bonded symbiotes rush down to the others in quick succession. And as the last one approaches, Shuri's Kimoyo bead vibrates to let her know the *Predator* is hovering right overhead.

She just has to keep the pack distracted for the twelve seconds it'll take for the miniature dome to deploy.

Glory to Bast, please let this work.

Name not Bast. But agree.

Shuri quickly taps the bead three times and then opens her mouth to speak . . . but the sounds that issue from her throat are like nothing she's ever heard before.

Not that she can't understand exactly what "Shurom" is communicating: "Brethren!" they say to the large group gathered all around them.

Four seconds down, Shuri thinks.

"Welcome to this great land—"

"NEW HOME!" a symbiote shout-growls from somewhere deep in the throng. Shurom spots him. He is *very* large and *very* menacing, with a many-fanged smile that's more *can't-wait-to-EAT-you* than *lovely-to-meet-you!*

Seven seconds down. More than halfway there.

"Actually, after spending significant time here, I feel that this planet is too . . . chaotic for our kind—"

"NEW HOOOOOOME!" the big guy shouts again. This time, the rest of the symbiote crowd begins to cheer . . .

Which is when Shuri makes a grave error: She looks up.

So they all do.

There's no mistaking the shimmery half sphere that is actively coming down around them like a glass jar over a gathering of bugs (which isn't wholly inaccurate). And in that final second before the dome touches ground, a terrifying tumult breaks loose.

"*FLEEEEE!*" one of them says from somewhere on the fringe of the mass.

And *flee* they do.

Or at least they try to. The force with which some of them smack into the dome is so intense, they get thrown backward through the air like the Vibranium-enhanced rubber balls Shuri used to toss against the palace wall to see how great a distance she could get them to rebound.

And they are *not* happy about it.

"TRAITORRRRR!" the big, scary one shouts, pointing at Shurom. (So much for a *new home* . . .)

And then he's rushing in her direction.

"Uhhhh . . . PLAN B, GUYS!" she shouts as loud as she can, hoping her team not only heard her but could understand what she said. Then she turns to run, but her symbiote stops her.

No *show fear!*

BUT I'M SCARED!

No *worry. I will handle.*

And before Shuri knows what's happening, her arm is up, and thick webbing is shooting out from some mysterious place beneath her Kimoyo bracelet.

It hits the big guy in the eyes and knocks him onto his back.

FWISH. FWISH. FWISH. FWISH.

One. Two. Three. Four more down, trying to claw the gunk off their faces.

Which is when Shuri notices more of them dropping in the same fashion. Spider-Man is also webbing them down left and right. He tosses the Frisbee, and a high-pitched whistling sound screeches through the air. A number of the beings immediately stop to cover their ears.

Why aren't they shooting it back at us? Shuri asks the symbiote.

No have webbing, the symbiote replies. *Venom adapt from host Spider-Man. Then share adaptation with me. Sole advantage. But too much webbing make weak—*

Spider-Man fires off a burst of web at Shuri, but thankfully, her symbiote's reflexes are quick as lightning. They do a double-backflip roll thing and land in a squat. "STOP! IT'S ME!" she shouts in his direction.

But of course it comes out in that wretched gravel voice.

CHANGE ME BACK TO ME! she shouts at the symbiote in her head.

And he must listen because Miles is suddenly so shocked, he pauses for a second too long and gets pummeled by a pair of unwebbed symbiotes.

"NO!" Shuri shouts. And then she's racing in Miles's direction as one of the black-clad alien creeps raises his hand into the air and extends his claws. Shuri shoots two bursts of web: one at the hand and one at his mouth. She flips and twists through the air and kicks the other one in the side of the head. But once her feet are back on the ground, she gets hit with a wave of vertigo.

Shuri spins in a quick circle. All around the enclosed field, her beloved friends and family are engaged in various styles of combat with their alien-possessed countrymen. T'Challa has taken on three at once. Okoye knocks one down with the handle of her long spear, and then whips around in a sweeping kick to take down another one. Ayo has just flipped one over her shoulder and blasted two others down with the gauntlets. Nakia runs up the trunk of the tree, does a backflip, and shoots the sonic blaster's silent sound beam at a group of seven while airborne. She lands on one's shoulders before dropping an elbow onto its head.

And then there's K'Marah. Who appears to be enjoying a nice piggyback ride until Shuri notices the Dora Karami has the symbiote in a choke hold with one arm and is rubbing the poison panther toy in its face with the opposite hand.

"Shuri! The big blast!" Spider-Miles says as a long string of web zips through the air from his wrist and attaches to a symbiote. When Miles pulls, the alien goes flying, and good ol' Spider-Man whips his body around in a wide loop, knocking at least a dozen of the others over like those red-and-white pins in that bizarre American game where a heavy ball is tossed down a greased lane.

Shuri lifts her arm to twist the right Kimoyo bead . . . but then stops. *Oh no*, she thinks. *When I do this,* you *will be blown off* me, she says to her own symbiote.

Princess too worried, the being responds.

And she is. Which feels odd considering how keen she was on the alien leaving her homeland and never returning.

Others teleport. Me wait for gem. Now press button.

So Shuri does.

And though she knows the frequency is too high for her *actual* ears to hear, the agony that hits the symbiote she's hosting is excruciating. It's as though the world around her is vibrating and spinning at the same time, and she's trying to swim through an ocean of the straight pins Clothier Lwazi uses when fitting Shuri for some ridiculous garment Mother will eventually force her to wear.

I have to stop it— she begins, but her extraterrestrial friend cuts her off.

No, he says. *Princess strong. Turn to maximum.*

Completely without her permission, Shuri's fingertips find the right Kimoyo bead and twist. Which makes it feel like thirty thousand sirens are going off inside her head at once. She squeezes her eyes shut and opens her mouth to scream.

Shuri has no idea how much time passes, but the next thing she knows, the symbiote's voice is saying

Goodbye, Princess and fading from her mind. The ache in her head begins to abate, though now she feels like she's going to lose her lunch and fall asleep simultaneously.

"Shuri, the vacuum!" K'Marah's voice says from somewhere far off.

The princess's hand drifts back to her bracelet, and she taps a bead—praying to Bast that it's the right one.

Then the world goes dark.

21

COMPLETION

When the princess opens her eyes, she's no longer on the plain. She props herself up on her elbows to look around . . . and finds herself in her bed.

Was that whole thing a dream?

Her bedroom door opens.

"Ah! You're awake!" Nakia says, walking over to place a cup of water on the princess's bedside table.

"Uhhh . . . what day is it?" Shuri says.

At this, Nakia laughs. "It's only been a few hours, Your Majesty."

"Oh. A few hours since . . . what precisely?"

"Ehh, nothing major," the Msingi replies with a smirk. "Just you freeing one hundred and eighty-three Wakandans from their alien captors, and subsequently suctioning what looked like a giant oil spill up into the belly of your Panther aircraft."

Shuri's head whips left and she locks eyes with her favorite Dora. "You mean it was all *real*?"

Nakia laughs again. "As real as the black eye your brother acquired in the mass brawl."

For the next who-knows-how-many-minutes, the beautiful warrior sits by Shuri's side, recounting all that transpired after Shuri's personal symbiote detached from her body and she fell unconscious. And she apparently wasn't the only one: "It was the strangest thing I have ever seen," Nakia says. "These black blobs vibrating like mad and then flying off their various hosts . . . who all looked around, very clearly con-fused, before collapsing the same way you did."

Medical personnel were dispatched and Nakia assures Shuri that the other hosts—who came from all over the nation—are perfectly fine, if not disoriented and convinced they were dreaming.

"You saved countless lives today, Your Majesty," Nakia continues. "You stepped out in courage and took a major risk, and it paid off. Again."

Spider-Miles, as it turns out, was whisked away

almost as soon as the fight was over. "The American spider hero received quite the royal transport treatment: T'Challa sent him home in the stealth jet."

"Wow," Shuri replies. T'Challa doesn't even allow *her* onto the stealth jet, and she's the one who invented it.

Nakia gives a brief recap of landing the *Predator* as instructed, using the remote that Shuri gave her.

But just before the princess can ask if a thermal scan was run on the cargo hold to make sure all (but one) of the symbiotes were gone, Nakia's bracelet rings.

When she taps the bead to accept the call, a silhouette of the queen mother's upper half appears in midair above her wrist. "Ah, the princess is awake, I see!" she says. *Over*enthusiastically. "Delightful! Nakia, please escort my daughter to the throne room as soon as possible. She has a visitor."

Shuri barely has the energy to keep her feet moving, let alone ponder over who this *visitor* might be . . .

But when she steps into the throne room and sees who is sitting beside Mother, the princess's mouth goes bone dry.

"We meet again!" M'Baku bellows. From the grin on his face, Shuri can tell he's up to no good . . . for *her* at least.

"Uhhhhh . . ." is all she can muster to say.

"M'Baku was kind enough to return this." Mother holds up one of the earrings that were gifted to the princess during her Tayari—the three-day rite of passage ceremony Wakandan girls go through at age twelve. Shuri's hands go to her earlobes . . . the left one is woefully empty.

"I sure hope all the *gadgets* you snuck into my domain were helpful in your 'conversation' with our Henbane. He is feeling much better, by the way." M'Baku glowers in Shuri's direction.

"Now, while I can appreciate your work in ridding our nation of those bizarre extraterrestrial invaders, and I cannot reprimand your Msingi for permitting you to embark on such a dangerous quest behind my back—again," Mother continues, "now that I know you visited the Jabari-Lands *and* violated their tech prohibition—"

"Let me guess," Shuri says, completely unfazed about cutting her mother off. (It's not as though the princess has anything to lose now, does she?) "I'm grounded."

Queen Ramonda smiles. "I am so glad we understand each other, Shuri."

MISSION LOG

I WOULD NEVER ALLOW MOTHER TO HEAR ME
SAY THIS, BUT ONE GOOD THING ABOUT BEING
"GROUNDED" IS THAT I HAVE ALL THE TIME
IN THE WORLD TO TWEAK AND INVENT AND
WORK ON VARIOUS UNFINISHED PROJECTS.

Like our security dome.

After the whole Battle of the Alien
Symbiote Horde thing, I checked the
Kimoyo Capture programming and discovered that the hole in the dome above the
Jabari-Lands was the result of there
being absolutely nothing Kimoyo connected in the entire region.

It might be said that this problem was
remedied through a series of beads that
happened to be "dropped" in various

mountain spots one night while I "dreamed" that I snuck out and was flying through the region on ropes of strange web-like material. (And I know this is a further violation of M'Baku's no-tech rules, but the safety of the entire nation is VERY clearly at stake.)

Only once the dome was complete did I present our symbiote with the nebular gem. Or perhaps I should say *Venbane*. Once our alien friend came to realize that, even with said gem, they wouldn't be able to return to their home planet—the hostility they were sure to face was quite the deterrent—he reconnected with Henbane, and the pair decided to just "pop" up wherever tickled their shared fancy.

K'Marah has clearly moved on: When I told her Henbane would be traveling the cosmos as the symbiote's host, she barely responded. "Great for him! Hey, look at the photograph Miles just sent me. He snapped it while swinging through New York City on his webs. Isn't he so talented?"

I simply rolled my eyes at that one.

Oddly enough, I *do*, in fact, miss the

symbiote. Having a companion inside my head to bounce ideas off of was nice for a time. I would never admit it aloud, but I am hoping that he eventually comes back—though also hoping the others stay far, far away forever. My biggest hope is that I'll be able to call to them like they said I could. Supposedly, hosting a symbiote creates a bond for as long as both entities are alive. I'd really like for them to come to one of the camps we'll be hosting at the Hive some four months from now . . .

Because that's the other thing. One day when Mother was out of the palace—shopping with Clothier Lwazi—T'Challa summoned me to the throne room.

My dear brother was so impressed by what we pulled off, he has decided to fully fund K'Marah's and my Run-The-World Camp. The first round of invitations has already gone out.

So there you have it. Wakanda is safe (and alien-free . . . for now, at least), whole, and beginning to take part in the affairs of the rest of the world. I am still not quite sure how I feel about all of it, but camp will certainly be fun . . .

If I can manage to stay un-grounded, that is.

I have given my Msingi my word that I will be on my best(ish) behavior.

For now, at least.

Princess Shuri signing off.

Wakanda forever.